MW00929754

KING OTTO'S CROWN

RICHARD ROTH

KING OTTO'S CROWN

RICHARD ROTH

Translated by Mary E. Ireland

G
GNESIO
BOOKS

King Otto's Crown by Richard Roth; translated by Mary E. Ireland.

This text was published in 1917 by Concordia Publishing House.

The original text of this book is in the public domain and may be freely used and copied.

This is a work of fiction.

All rights reserved.

Additions to the original text Copyright © 2017 Gnesio Books.

G

Gnesio Books
gnesiobooks@gmail.com

First Gnesio Edition

⚹ A Glimpse into the Past ⚹

MANY YEARS AGO, in the reign of Henry I of Germany, Hengist and Keringer, brothers of eleven and twelve years, were playing about a small lake at the foot of the Harz Mountains in Saxony.

It was a bright afternoon in early winter, and the snowy peaks of the mountains gleamed in the sun-light, their shadows and those of the forest trees making miniature copies of themselves upon the surface of the ice-bound lake.

Beautiful was this lake in summer, its ripples sparkling in the sunbeams, and wild flowers blooming luxuriantly upon its banks, but equally appreciated by the boys in winter.

Healthy, bright, handsome boys they were, straight as pine-trees on the mountainside, with ruddy cheeks, bright blue eyes, and blond hair, which fell in ringlets nearly to their waists from under their bearskin caps, that being the custom in those early times.

"Keringer!" called Hengist, "father warned us to be careful and not go too near that part of the lake where the warm stream runs, for the ice is thin and the water deep."

"I will be careful," replied the boy, but a moment later the ice cracked, and he dropped into the water, but fortunately succeeded in throwing his arms out over the ice, which kept him from going under. The ice broke under the weight of his arms, he pushed on to a firmer place; again the ice broke, and he was compelled to move along.

"Do not be frightened, brother," called Hengist, "I will shout for help until someone comes!" and this he did at the top of his clear voice. But there was no response; only the melancholy *hiah! hiah!* of an eagle circling overhead, breaking the silence of the secluded place.

It was indeed an unlikely spot to get assistance; there was a narrow, winding, rough road down the valley, but it was seldom that anyone passed that way during the winter; and although the tower and battlements of the ancient castle where they lived were plainly in view, it was scarcely possible for a boy's voice to reach anyone there.

Keringer's body was chilled and his arms lamed by the strain upon them, and he was almost despairing of rescue; but Hengist continued his call for help, turning his head in all directions, hoping someone would hear, when a strong manly voice responded, and a hunter forced his way through the undergrowth of the forest.

He was tall and of distinguished and commanding presence, and was in full hunting costume. His cap was of costly otter-skin, his hunting-jacket of valuable fur; slung over his shoulder was a cross-bow and a quiver of arrows, a large, bright hunting-knife was in his belt, and in his right hand was a spear.

He saw at a glance the danger, the need, and the remedy, and called in a cheery voice:

"Hold on a moment longer, my boy, and you will soon be on safe ground."

He bent down a stout limb of a sapling, and with his hunting-knife cut it on each side; then with a twist of his strong hand he broke it off, trimming off the branches as he hurried to the lake.

"Now, my boy, this strong pole will save you," he said as he pushed it toward him; "place it across the hole in the ice, grasp it with both hands, and push it along toward the shore. If the ice breaks, it won't matter; the pole will keep you from sinking. Push it along until the ice will not break, then it will be strong enough to bear your weight; climb out, and with God's help you will be safe on shore."

Keringer obeyed, and a moment later a strong hand drew him to a place beside him.

"Now run home as quickly as you can to change your wet clothing so you won't take cold. But first tell me your names, and where you live."

"Hengist and Keringer, and our home is Castle Eberstein," said Hengist, pointing to it; "and we thank you for saving Keringer," he added.

"Now goodbye, and I hope we will meet again. I often hunt in this forest!" The young man now turned to go.

"Will you please tell us your name?" asked Hengist, and both boys listened eagerly for the reply.

"Oh, that will be a fine conundrum for you to guess by the time we meet again," he replied with a merry nod. "Goodbye! Goodbye!" and he disappeared amid the bushes of the forest.

Fine, handsome, well-bred boys! he said to himself as he hurried to join his fellow-huntsmen. *It would have been a sad affair had one been drowned. Thank God that I heard the call before he sank under the ice!*

This friend in need was Prince Otto, son of King Henry I of Saxony, who was the first emperor to be accepted by the whole body of German people, and was looked upon as the founder of the German Empire.

King Henry, his queen, Matilda, and his court were at his castle at Quedlinburg, in Saxony, at that time, which was but a few miles from the lake and the great forest.

In those days the king had no fixed homes, but marched through the empire from one palace or castle to another, and wherever he happened to be, he must be the judge of all doubtful or contested points among his subjects.

Immense forests — also the property of the reigning monarch — covered at that time a great part of the land, and in them roamed the wolf, the bear, the bison, the elk, and wild boars, which furnished amusement and food for huntsmen.

It was in tracking one of these animals that Prince Otto had heard the call for help, and saved a human life; and feeling happy over it, he rejoined his companions, while the boys ran down the valley to Castle Eberstein.

❧ A Visit to King Otto ❧

FOUR YEARS PASSED AWAY. It was now May, and Hengist and Keringer had grown almost to man's height. They were in their hunting costume, and were again by the lake in the valley, now in its summer beauty.

The mountain streams were foaming and gurgling on the way to the ravines below, the birds in the forest were singing and chirping as they darted about, and a nest of young eagles on a mountain height clamored as if having a craving for food, but nothing to satisfy it.

A wild cat sprang from one high point to another in search of prey, not fearing the bows and arrows of the boys in the valley, who were glancing up at it while wending their way through bushes, briars, and stumps, not heeding hindrances.

"I wonder why father does not come," said Keringer when they reached the entrance of a ravine; "he said he would meet us here, where last evening we saw the track of a bear, and he never has failed us."

The place had indeed a wild aspect; rocks towered high above them, and cast dark shadows upon the winding path between.

They had been there but a few minutes, when they heard snarling and scuffling, the sound of conflict and calls for help.

"It is the bear!" exclaimed Hengist. "someone has wounded it and is now in danger."

With their hunting-knives in hand they ran up the ravine and found a hunter on his back upon the ground, and the paw of a huge bear upon his breast, which prevented him from using his hunting-knife, and he was at the mercy of the infuriated beast.

He had speared it, but not in a vital part; it had rushed upon him and thrust him to the ground.

The boys heard the call and ran to his assistance just as the animal had sunk his teeth in the shoulder of the prostrate man; a moment more of time would have been too late to save him, but that moment was used by the boys in plunging their hunting-knives into the heart of the bear. He relaxed his hold, rolled over, and the outstretched hands of his deliverers helped the hunter to his feet.

"You came at the right time," he said gratefully; "another moment and it would have been too late. I thank God, who sent you as His instruments to save me from a terrible death."

"We must look at your wounded shoulder," said Hengist; "see, it is bleeding."

"My thick hunting-jacket has kept me from suffering much injury, I think." When the boys removed it, they found two cuts made by the teeth, but not so deep and dangerous as they had feared.

"I came off well," remarked the hunter; "had it been my throat, I could not have lived. You boys have saved my life, and from my heart I thank you."

"You saved my life," said Keringer; "now I rejoice that I have aided in saving yours."

"I saved your life? When and where?" He looked inquiringly at them. "Why, I do not know you, have never seen you until now."

"But *we* know *you*; do you not remember Hengist and Keringer? You saved the life of Keringer when he broke through the ice on the lake. He would have been drowned had you not pushed a strong pole to him and told him how to use it," said Hengist cheerily.

"Can it be possible? I would not have supposed that you could have grown to nearly men's size in those four years. I certainly did not remember you."

"It is no wonder that you did not know us; you scarcely gave us time to thank you," laughed Keringer.

"Hengist and Keringer, are you there?" called a strong voice at the mouth of the ravine.

"Yes, father, we are here"; and in response to the hunter's questioning glance, they told him that their father had come out with them the evening before to hunt the bear of which they had seen tracks.

"Oh, boys, the recklessness of coming into the ravine in search of the bear!" rebuked their father the moment he caught sight of them.

"But we have him, father," they called joyously.

They were soon joined by a large, strong-looking man, but lame, and with lines of care upon his fine face.

"Oh, now I see," he continued, turning to the hunter, "you have killed him, and the boys came to rejoice with you."

"No, your sons killed him, and I have to thank them for my being alive at this moment. I am with a party of huntsmen, and we saw traces of a bear and parted to go in different directions to search for him. I saw him enter this ravine, and threw the spear which wounded him; he turned, threw me down, and planted his huge foot upon my breast, and I could not move to reach for my knife. I would have been killed had not your sons come at the proper moment to stab him and save me; I owe my life to them."

"They merely did their duty," replied the father, yet with a look of pride he gazed upon his handsome sons, who had saved a life.

"I think you are a stranger in this region," he said, turning to the hunter, "I never saw you in this forest, I am quite sure."

"It has only happened that we have never met, for I frequently hunt in this forest."

"This is the kind huntsman that saved me from drowning, father, the time I broke through the ice," explained Keringer.

"Oh, is it possible that at last I see him whom I have long wished to see and thank for his deed of great kindness to me and mine? These boys are the tie that binds me to life; I have had many trials, and they are my stay and comfort. My name is Gerhard von Stein, and I have been a soldier."

"I can well believe you were a soldier, and a brave one. I will walk along with you on your way to your home, and you can tell me what is agreeable to you to tell, and withhold what you prefer to keep to yourself."

"There is nothing to keep back, and I will tell all there is to tell. Boys," he continued, turning to them, "cover the bear with pine branches, and tomorrow we will bring tools and take off his skin, his hind legs, and his paws." Saying this, he and the stranger took their way down the path through the valley.

"In the year 924," the father of the boys said to the stranger as they slowly walked along toward Eberstein Castle, "a wild horde of Hungarians broke into our part of Saxony like an overwhelming flood, and King Henry gathered as quickly as possible an army to combat them. I am a soldier of a long line of knights, to which my wounds and scars bear witness, and I would have laid down my life for King Henry. A small castle on the river Unstrut was my ancestral home; there with my beloved wife and bright, beautiful little boy, Arnulf, nearly two years old, we lived so happily that to leave it to go to war was a trial.

"There was no great battle with the Huns, for our army was too small in numbers to risk waging war with such an overpowering horde; but there were many light skirmishes between them and King Henry's loyal men at the fortress of Werla at the foot of the Harz Mountains.

"During the last one of these skirmishes, an arrow grazed my eye, and I lost the sight of it; and a spear wounded my knee, which caused lameness.

"For several weeks I lay at the fortress of Werla, unable to join in any action, and in the meantime King Henry concluded a truce with the Hungarians for nine years' duration.

"With one of my faithful retainers I set out for my castle, rejoicing that after so many weeks of absence I would be at my home with my wife and child, and could by my presence add to their comfort and happiness.

"We traveled along hopefully, and my surprise and bewilderment was beyond expression when, from the top of a hill, I saw no sign of my home; the Hungarians had been there, and my castle was a heap of ruined walls and ashes.

"I would have fallen from my horse had not my faithful servant prevented it, and we stayed at the place which had been my home.

"One attendant had remained there, in case I returned, to tell me that my wife had come here to Eberstein Castle, which was the ancestral home of her family, and was occupied by her brother, the last one left of her father's family and he in feeble health, but who gave her a hearty welcome.

"Her heart was broken over the loss of our little Arnulf whom the Hungarians had stolen; and in my own deep grief for the loss of our boy I strove to comfort her.

"We would have been far happier to know that he was lying in his little grave, instead of living in the hands of that wild, lawless people; but we bore our trouble as best we could.

"My poor brother-in-law was our comfort while he lived, but he passed away the next year, and later God sent us these two dear sons. When Keringer was five years old, my wife passed away; and we have lived at the old Castle Eberstein with our faithful retainers, trying to bear the loss of wife and mother as is our duty and in obedience to God's will."

"It has indeed been a sore trial to you," remarked the hunter, "but, Gerhard von Stein, did you never apply to King Henry for reimbursement for the loss of your property and the injury to you caused by wounds?"

"I never thought of doing anything of the kind. We should only think of the honor and freedom which our beloved Germany enjoys. That is the offering which is required and expected of all the sons of the fatherland. It would have been impossible for our late noble king to pay all his soldiers who lost property, and for injuries received in fighting for our country's honor."

The shades of evening were drawing on, the song of birds in the forest had nearly ceased, and the hunter, taking a little silver horn held by a cord about his neck, placed it to his lips and gave a clear call that echoed through the forest.

"My hunting companions will now join me," he said, as he shook the hands of his companions. "We have come to the parting of the ways, but I hope we will meet again; till then farewell." Stepping lightly over the trunk of a fallen tree, he disappeared in the forest.

"Oh, father, you forgot to ask his name," exclaimed Hengist.

"Yes, it was in my mind several times, and I don't see why I could not ask it. Kind and agreeable as was his manner, there was something in it that restrained me."

"Something majestic," suggested Keringer.

"That is exactly the word," said his father, "majestic"; and the three passed on to the ancient fortress.

One morning, several days later, a horseman of knightly appearance passed through the courtyard gate of Castle Eberstein.

A helmet graced his head, a chained armor protected his body, a sword in its scabbard was at his side, a poniard in his girdle, and over his shoulder hung a shield.

The stamping of his horse brought Hengist and Keringer quickly to see the visitor, and speeding to tell a servant to attend to the horse, they sped to their father.

Gerhard was pointing arrows, but came quickly to welcome the unknown guest.

"My name is Kabald, and I am chamberlain of His Majesty King Otto," explained the visitor in a courtly manner, as he took the seat that Gerhard von Stein gave him.

Hengist took off the helmet, and Keringer brought a footstool; then the two sons took a seat beside the father to learn the occasion of the visit.

"I am sent by King Otto to you, Gerhard von Stein, and to your sons Hengist and Keringer, to tell you that it has come to his knowledge that your good and brave sons have saved a hunter in the forest from the teeth and claws of a bear, thus keeping him from losing his life.

"Also it has come to the knowledge of King Otto that you, Gerhard von Stein, have done the fatherland great service, and with much loss to you. My royal master, in view of these services, sends his personal thanks to you, and the aim of my visit is to invite all three of you to come to his castle at Quedlinburg, where he is staying at present, and where he would like to meet you, if you have no objection to the long ride. I have a friend on the way whom I would like to visit for a half hour, but it will not hinder you on your journey, for I have the swiftest horse in the stables of the king's Marshall, and can easily catch up with you before you reach Quedlinburg. What is your answer, Gerhard von Stein?"

"What the king commands, is the duty of myself and my sons to obey. But first your horse must have oats, and you some refreshment, which I offer freely, though I must add that it will be very plain."

Keringer ran out to give both orders, and in a little while a meal was upon the table for four, simple indeed, black bread, stewed wild plums, and roast bear-meat. The guest expressed himself as being well-satisfied with the meal, and especially was he pleased to know that the meat was from the hind leg of the bear which the boys had killed in the forest, thus saving the hunter from the teeth and claws of the infuriated animal.

An hour later the four rode out the courtyard and over the drawbridge on their way to visit King Otto.

The horses of the father and sons were old, and their progress was not to be compared with the swift movement of the chamberlains; and when he branched off to visit his friend, they saw that it would be no trouble for him to catch up with them again should his call extend over the half hour.

"I well remember my last visit to Quedlinburg," remarked the father as they traveled along side by side; "it was just eighteen years ago. King Henry knew that a great injustice had been done me, and he gave me an audience without delay.

"Queen Matilda was present, and also their little son Otto, now our king; he has worn the crown since his father's death in 936, and in the three years he has ruled he has won the love of his subjects; for, like his father and mother, he is sincere and good. I have never seen him since he was a child, for there was nothing to call me to Quedlinburg when the king and his court paid a visit there."

"Father, it would be pleasant to hear you tell of the kings Henry and Otto; we so love to hear of people who have ruled over our beloved fatherland."

To Gerhard von Stein nothing was more agreeable than to converse with his sons, and to listen to their opinions, freely expressed to one who had always been as an elder brother in their secluded life at the ancient fortress, and after a moment's reflection as to the place to begin, he proceeded to tell them how the line was changed from the Carlovingian dynasty to the imperial House of Saxony.

3

✴ Father and Sons on Their Short Journey ❧

IT WILL NOT BE NECESSARY, my sons, to go farther back in German history for our short journey to Quedlinburg, than to King Conrad I, who, when about to pass from earth, called his brother Eberhard, who, as heir to the German throne, would have worn the crown of the kingdom of Germany.

"Dear brother," said Conrad feebly, "I realize that I must soon leave the world, and I long for the best welfare of the fatherland. This is a mighty kingdom; we have cities and waterways, we have a population that can afford great armies in the field, and everything else that belongs to a kingly country; but in real ability, which brings success, we are lacking. These advantages and abilities to procure success are possessed in a high degree by Henry, Duke of Saxony, once our enemy and antagonist. Upon this great man, Duke Henry of Saxony, rests the prosperity of the German kingdom; therefore in these, the last hours of my life upon earth, I ask you to grant my heartfelt wish, and demand that Henry be my successor. Dear brother, I implore you to renounce your right and claim to the throne for the sake of the wellbeing of the kingdom. When my eyes are closed in death, take to him the tokens of kingship and royal dignity, the crown and the crown jewels, bring the Saxon duke here, and make him your friend. Tell him that I chose him as my successor, and the last wish of a dying man should be fulfilled."

"And did Eberhard do this?" asked both boys eagerly.

"He did, and you can well understand, my dear sons,

that to Eberhard these words caused deep disappointment and real grief. But truly great he proved to be; he made the sacrifice for the sake of his brother and his beloved country, and Henry of Saxony became King of Germany.

"'I know well,' said Eberhard, 'that a king's crown is a heavy burden, yet I will give the German prince my allegiance, and what strength I possess to the kingdom.' And he kept his word.

"King Henry I was of noble appearance. I would give much to have had you see him; tall and stately, with broad shoulders and straight limbs and handsome features. Courage and determination shone in his fine, clear eyes. Elastic in his movements, splendid of form, he was a king from the crown of his head to the soles of his feet.

"Yet, in spite of all these endowments, only the Saxons and the Franconians acknowledged him as their king. The Swabians, Bavarians, and the Lothringians refused to accept him. But there came punishment for their injustice, for against Burchard, the Swabian duke, Henry brought an army unexpectedly, and in a short battle overthrew him, and from that time he was a faithful vassal of King Henry.

"Then King Henry brought an army against Arnulf of Bavaria; and a terrible battle was fought. The king was deeply distressed at witnessing the terrible fight between German brothers, and he sent for Arnulf to have a conversation with him.

"'Why did you strive against the will of God?' he asked. 'Who gave me the crown, if it was not God? It was He who put it into the heart of the late king and the bishop who chose me for your king. Had God put you upon the throne, no one would have been more willing to give you allegiance than I; it was only because God willed it that I took up the burden of the crown. How will you answer to God for this shedding of innocent blood? How will you answer to your conscience for your jealous, envious insubordination, causing brave German soldiers to give up their lives, brother fighting against brother, and leaving the frontiers of the kingdom unprotected against outside enemies?'

"Arnulf recognized the truth of this, and in real repentance and submission he became faithful in his allegiance to the noble king.

"Henry had won the battle by force of arms, but a greater one by discreet admonition and wise handling of a difficult subject.

"The Lothringians were the next to be taken in hand, and I had part in all the battles against them. Then King Henry had to turn his attention to outside enemies, of whom the most dangerous were the Hungarians, a wild, plundering horde of horsemen.

"They knew the kingdom's weakness after their fierce battles among themselves, and believed that an invasion would not meet with much resistance, and like an impetuous flood they broke over the borders, filling the hearts of the people with terror and anxiety.

"They were inherited enemies of the fatherland, and were indeed to be feared for their wonderful skill in using their swords, lances, spears, and bows and arrows. Standing on the backs of their horses, or leaning over their sides, the weapons of these wild people seldom missed their mark.

"Their horses were small and marvels of endurance; and with deafening cries these wild horsemen made an onslaught, and if not having the success they wished, they took apparent flight; the attacked would follow, whereupon they would turn, and use their weapons with terrible havoc, sparing no one, not even women and children. Old men were killed or taken prisoners, and homes were robbed of everything that could be carried away.

"In one short battle with them I was wounded in the knee. I was in the fortress of Werla, when, one day, our soldiers came jubilantly in, bringing as a prisoner a young Hungarian prince.

"The enemy offered a high price for his ransom, but Henry made his demand, which was a nine years' cessation of hostilities; and he would accept nothing else as ransom for the Hungarian prince. It was accepted by them, and for nine years our kingdom was secure from their depredations.

"At that time our country had very few cities and fortresses. Only on the shores of the Rhine and the

Danube, and beyond these rivers, where the Romans had ruled, could these be found, and most of them were in ruins.

"The people, as a rule, lived in small dwellings, and as there were but few villages, the country stood open to the enemy, for the inhabitants were so scattered that they could not unite to protect it.

"Henry did much to improve this state of things; he encouraged his subjects to form villages and strongholds, that they might have gathering-places for their own protection.

"There was also a change as to defense. In all the battles with the Hungarians, the Germans were in the minority; and it became King Henry's care to strengthen his army. Moreover, the Hungarians were on horseback, while the Germans were on foot and heavily burdened with their weapons, and he resolved to better this during the nine years; and he succeeded.

"In the meantime, the time of truce was nearly out, and that the Hungarians would not wait long was known to every German, and the king called them together in order to come to an understanding as to what was the best plan to take in case of an attack.

"'As you all know,' he said to the throng of gathered soldiers, 'in contrast to our former troubles and disorder in our beloved land, we have for nearly nine years been free from the burdens of inward feuds and open war. But against the Hungarians we must soon be at all times prepared; for very soon I must free them from their oath, and again the Church of God and His servants will be robbed and plundered, and nothing will be left them but, perhaps, their lives. Weigh this matter well in your minds, and decide upon the best course to be taken'; and he waited for their answer. All agreed that the hereditary enemy should be quelled.

"'Will you take oath that you will stand by me though it may cost your lives?' With uplifted hand each took the oath.

"Oh, boys," continued Gerhard, "it went through my heart that I, a poor crippled man, could not take part against the foul enemy of the fatherland. My sword must rust in its scabbard, while my fellow-soldiers were doing their duty.

Children, it was a trial hard to bear.

"As soon as the nine years were past, messengers were sent by the Hungarians requesting tribute-money. To their astonishment and anger they had to return with empty hands. A few weeks after, they came like an overwhelming swarm of grasshoppers over Thuringia and Saxony.

"King Henry hurriedly gathered a large army of horsemen and gave summons to battle. Fortunately the great army of the Hungarians could not find sufficient food in Thuringia, and they agreed that a part of the army should remain there, and another part go westward; and there the King and his company met them and nearly exterminated them. Then he and his army battled with the other part. He told his soldiers to look to God for assistance, assuring them that the Almighty would be with them in their endeavors to save their homes and their country from destruction.

"The hearts of his soldiers swelled with courage and hope. Their beloved king was with them, now in one part of the field, now in another, and always with his banner bearing the emblem of the archangel Gabriel.

"The Hungarians were bewildered at seeing the difference between this warfare and that of nine years before. They took to flight, and their camp and its possessions, and their prisoners fell into the hands of King Henry."

4

⚜ A Pleasant Surprise ⚜

ERHARD VON STEIN HAD FINISHED his account of King Henry I and his troubles with the Hungarians, when horses' hoofs were heard coming at a rapid pace, and the chamberlain joined them just as the turrets and battlements of Quedlinburg Castle came into view.

They rode in company over the drawbridge, and entered the great courtyard. The statue of a Saxon warrior guarded the entrance with sword in scabbard, spear in hand, a shield held by a band over the shoulder, betokening, as it were, that it were impossible for any except invited guests to enter there.

But Gerhard von Stein and his sons were not only invited guests, but were brought there by the chamberlain of King Otto.

Servants came to take charge of the horses, and Kabald conducted the guests through the grand entrance into a large apartment, evidently the favorite room of a hunter.

"Here you will wait," he said, "to be received by our gracious King Otto. I will tell him that you are here," and he left the apartment.

"I was received by King Henry in this room," remarked the father; and a look of sorrow shadowed his face at the remembrance of one who had passed from earth four years before, in the year 936; and the places that knew him upon earth would know him no more.

Upon the wainscoted walls were great antlers of deer and elks, horns of the chamois, and tusks of wild boars and bisons, as well as hunting-weapons of all kinds, each and all full of interest to the boys.

They were still gazing at them when a man's footsteps were heard in the corridor. The door opened and the hunter they had met in the ravine stood before them, wearing the hunting-garb he had worn the day they killed the bear and saved his life; and they supposed he had come to announce the king.

"King Otto greets his beloved friends of the ravine," he said as with a friendly smile he grasped their hands and shook them cordially.

The father bowed respectfully, and the boys followed his example, though bewildered by the surprise, feeling as though it were all a dream.

That they had saved the life of the ruler of the great German Empire seemed too wonderful to be true.

"Yes, boys, I am the hunter whose life you saved from the claws and teeth of the bear, and through God's providence I owe my being yet upon the earth to you.

"And you, Gerhard von Stein, through your unpremeditated history of your experiences and losses caused by the war, gave such heartfelt expression to the love you bore my dear father and our beloved country that I wish to make some recompense to you and your boys for what you have done for me and mine.

"On the Lippe River there is a property belonging to me called Hartrun. It has a large, substantial castle, many acres of cultivated land, plenty of fruit, a great stretch of woodland, or forest, in which are deer and other wild animals for food and for sport in hunting. This property I give to you and your sons for all times, and the deed for it is ready for you."

With these words he took from a niche in the wall an inlaid casket, unlocked it, and took from it a roll of parchment which he placed in the hand of Gerhard.

"I cannot express my gratitude and happiness in receiving this gift," said his guest, his lips trembling with emotion; "it is a royal gift, worthy the great heart of the giver."

"There is another fine property near Hartrun, which belongs to my brother, Duke Henry of Bavaria; it is called Castle Beleke, and is occupied only by the steward Ruppert and his son Wido; the boy is about the age of your sons, is a good, sensible boy, and will be excellent company for them. The two places are not far apart, and the two forests join."

"Thank you again and again," said Gerhard; "it is indeed a blessing to have our own home and land."

"It is to you that thanks are due and to your sons; had it not been for them, I would not be here to make the gift. And now my chamberlain will take you to have some refreshments after your ride."

It was a luxurious meal to which Kabald conducted them, and was heartily enjoyed. Then the chamberlain took them to the stables, where the coachman and other servitors awaited them, and they were shown three fine horses, two with black, glossy coats and one an equally glossy chestnut.

"What splendid horses!" exclaimed the boys in a breath.

"Are you really pleased with them?" smiled the chamberlain.

"Who could help being pleased; it must be a joy to pet this lovely one"; and he patted its soft mane.

"That joy can be yours; for the two belong to you boys to choose for yourselves between them, and the chestnut is for your father."

It, too, was a fine animal, but not so fleet as the blacks. All, however, were gentle and well trained.

"If you intend to go soon to Hartrun, the three horses will be taken there by order of the king," continued the chamberlain; "if not, they will be taken to the fortress. It rests entirely with you."

"It will better prove our keen appreciation of his majesty's gifts for us to go to Hartrun as quickly as possible," replied Gerhard; and thanking the chamberlain for his care and attention, the three happy recipients of the valuable gifts set out for the old fortress.

The gift of Hartrun was strong evidence of the generosity of the king as well as his gratitude, and, in compliment to the donor, Gerhard and his sons lost no time in exchanging their home in the dilapidated fortress for the comparatively new and substantial Hartrun Castle.

There was now no care in the heart of the father for the future of his sons; and the old soldier's heart thrilled at the thought that there was not only a settled home, but life would be full of interest in that spot. They now had a forest where they could roam at will as in the former home, so lost nothing in that respect, and gained in many others.

At one time there was no communication between Hartrun and Beleke Castles, for the owners, King Otto and his brother Henry, Duke of Bavaria, were enemies; but the wall which separated the forests that there might be no communication and no evidence of friendship between them, was still there, although peace had been apparently established between them.

The new owners of Hartrun had been there but a short time, when, one afternoon, they heard, on the other side of the token of the brother's enmity, the bellowing of dogs. A deer sprang over the wall and fell near the spot where Hengist and Keringer were standing. An arrow was in the poor animal's breast, and it did not rise, but lay there panting with pain and fright, while the hounds belonging to Hartrun bellowed with delight as they sniffed about the fallen deer. Presently two hunters appeared on the other side of the wall.

One of them was a tall, strong, middle-aged man, with gray hair and of soldier-like appearance; the other, a boy of about nineteen, with a fine, intelligent cast of countenance, both with spears, bows and arrows, and knives.

"The deer belongs to the fellow that lives at Hartrun," said the older man with a look of disappointment that it had jumped over the wall and he could not claim it. "Wait a moment, and I will silence the dogs," and he took an arrow from his quiver and was about to shoot when the young man grasped his arm.

"What have the poor dogs done that you are willing to kill them, father?" he said.

"What is that to you, Wido? Let go of my arm this minute!" But the boy would not release his clasp, and at that moment Gerhard von Stein, who had heard the bellowing, joined his sons.

"We live at Castle Hartrun," said Gerhard. "We were hunting in the forest and shot at the deer. Was it your arrow or ours that struck it?"

"It does not matter whose arrow struck it, it fell on your side. But I believe it is our deer, for it was in hiding for three hours where you could not have seen it, and my son sent the arrow that wounded it."

"I sent my arrow from a distance," said Keringer, "but I think I wounded the deer in the neck."

"Is that so? Do you, smart Aleck, think so little of my skill as a hunter as to believe that I missed my aim? You do not know that my arrow will go within a hair's breadth of' the mark."

"Do not begin a quarrel with our new neighbor, father," said Wido. "We both know that the deer came from the forest, and none of us knows whether it was from the Hartrun or the Beleke side. My suggestion would be to share the deer with our neighbor."

"Your son speaks wisely and justly," said Gerhard, "and it is a credit to his good heart and kind feelings to strangers. If you agree to that, Steward Ruppert, we will be well-satisfied; but if you believe that it was not my son's arrow, but yours, that killed it, we will give it up to you without a word of objection."

"I see that you are trying by your generosity to shame me. But you have reckoned without your host; I will not deny that it was in your part of the forest where he was feeding, and it was in your part of it where it was hidden; so the deer is yours. But look well and see if there is not an arrow wound in one of his hind legs, for I declare by St. Augustine that my arrow hit the deer as it jumped over the wall, which my gracious Duke Henry had built between the forests. But remember this; no one of you will go unpunished if you trespass over this wall."

"I could bid defiance to your insolence if I thought it worth the trouble," replied von Stein, his face flushing with anger. "Your son is far the more sensible of the two, and shows by his manner that he does not side with you. He knows that the right is on our side. But I do not wish to have any strife between us. Our superiors are at peace with each other, why should we not be good friends?"

"Peace indeed!" laughed Ruppert scornfully. "The only peace between two rulers is the will of the stronger; the other must follow in his footsteps. Where his opponent has luck, peace is only on the outside, and the world believes that all is well between them."

"That is no concern of ours," replied Gerhard; "and if you have a feeling of bitterness in your heart against us, that is no reason for us to feel that way toward you. We desire to have peace and good will, such as there should be between neighbors; but if Hartrun is such a thorn in your side, we will make this low wall the boundary line between us, and not to cross it will be my care and that of my sons."

Saying this, the new owner of Hartrun turned away, accompanied by Hengist and Keringer, each nodding a farewell to Wido.

"I am sorry that Steward Ruppert harbors such a feeling against us," remarked von Stein as they walked toward their home; "his face is not that of an evil-hearted man. He seems to be strictly obedient to duty, but he entertains the foolish idea that we are enemies."

"Wido seems to be friendly toward us," commented Hengist. "I like him, and I would be glad to have him as a friend."

"He is a fine boy, I am sure," agreed his father. "He has a truthful, clear gaze, pleasant manners, and, I think, is truly honorable and just. I would be very glad if you could be friends with him; he would be a helpful companion."

Just then the two dogs raised their heads and barked angrily.

"What is it, Risk and Rust?" said Keringer. "What animal is it you are scenting that does not please you?"

"It is not an animal, but a person," said his father. "I was told by the steward at Hartrun that it is a peculiarity of these dogs that they scent a person that is following in one's tracks." A little later they heard some footsteps upon the dry leaves and branches in the forest.

"Will you people of Hartrun halt a minute?" called a young buoyant voice, and Wido joined them, panting from his swift run through the forest.

"I wish to say that I am sorry that my father spoke as he did to you. He is a good, kind man, but he always speaks that way to one who is on the king's side instead of that of Duke Henry. For this reason, and that alone, he is angry with his twin brother, who is keeper of King Otto's forest at Merseburg. To tell you how it all came about would be quite a long story."

"We would like to hear it, Wido, if you have no objections to telling it."

"Yes, tell us," exclaimed his sons eagerly; and Wido was pleased to comply.

"We are Germans," he said, "and until the year 933 we lived in Hungary where my father was forester and hunter for a rich Hungarian who had a large estate. There my father and mother were happy and contented, and to-day he would be glad to return to Hungary. In the year 933, as you all know, there was a cessation of hostilities for nine years, and as soon as this truce period was at an end, the Hungarians swarmed over the border and attacked the Germans. There was a terrible battle at Riade, and the Hungarians were driven out of Germany. In wild haste those who escaped death returned to their homes, and ever since have been bitter in their hatred against the Germans living in their country. To the great distress of my parents the rich employer of my father was killed at the battle of Riade, and we had no protector whatever, and our lives were in danger.

"My mother had died, and my father decided to return to Germany, and with a small Hungarian horse and a poor little wagon, we started, taking with us the little money and clothing and the few articles that could be put in the wagon.

"We had not yet reached the border when we were attacked by four Hungarian robbers. My father is a very strong man, and knew how to handle weapons, but he was overpowered and I, but a boy, was of no help to him. We lost all we possessed. Father received some dangerous wounds, and we were compelled to walk to a small village, where the people gave us food, and we rested for a few days.

"My father was so exhausted from suffering great pain, loss of sleep, and physical exertion that after a walk of a few days since leaving the village, he was not able to rise from the bed of pine branches and leaves that I made for him. He believed that his end had come, and commended me to the care of a merciful God.

"But help was near, and such help as we had never imagined; for three horsemen appeared from the depths of the forest where they had been hunting, and one of them, a distinguished and handsome young man, stepped from his horse and stood beside my father.

"He saw the miserable condition, listened to our story, and sent us to his hunting-lodge not far away, to remain as long as we wished. Father was ill for weeks, and every comfort that could be had was provided for him.

"We found the young nobleman to be Prince Henry, now Duke Henry of Bavaria, and I cannot tell you of our gratitude to him for all he did for us; and we will be true to him to our dying day.

"You will see that it was only natural that, when the strife came between Duke Henry and his brother Otto for the crown of Germany, we were on the side of King Henry — such he was in our estimation, for my father firmly believes that he is the rightful heir to the crown which is now worn by King Otto.

"It is true that Otto is the elder son, but when he was born, his father, King Henry, was only Duke of Saxony, and when Prince Henry was born, his father was King of Germany, so Duke Henry of Bavaria was entitled to succeed his father as king. For this reason my father hates King Otto as one who wears a crown which rightfully belongs to his brother Henry. Therefore, anyone who is a friend of King Otto is a personal enemy of my father."

"But if ever a king had a right to his crown, that king is Otto," said Gerhard von Stein; "for his father, King Henry, when about to depart this life, appointed him as his successor, and no thoughtful person can be in doubt as to which side is right."

"I entirely agree with you," said Wido, "but nothing could change my father's opinion; and what I have said to you is to explain to you his reason for not wishing to be friendly."

"His love and loyalty to Duke Henry speaks well for him," commented von Stein; "it would be a dishonorable man indeed who could forget what the young nobleman did for him, and I honor him for it."

"Yes; Duke Henry not only saved his life, but afterward gave him the stewardship of Beleke Castle and its belongings; yet, if my father did not at heart believe that he is the true heir of the crown of Germany, these advantages would have no weight with him, for he is the soul of honor."

"I believe you," agreed Gerhard heartily; "his countenance is proof enough." Here the conversation ended, and they separated, each going to his home.

5

⚜ Treason against the King ⚜

THE FIRST WINTER had been pleasantly spent at Hartrun by Gerhard von Stein and his sons, and now it was three days before Easter, 941. They had heard through Wido that great preparations for the Easter festival were going on at Beleke Castle, for Duke Henry of Bavaria was coming to spend the holidays there, and would bring with him a number of distinguished guests.

The von Stein boys were glad to hear of this, and hoped to get a chance to see the young duke, for they believed he must resemble his brother, King Otto, Wido having described him as tall and slender, with blond hair worn in ringlets, and dark, expressive eyes. In his opinion he was very handsome. He might have added that Duke Henry was active, energetic, and restless, and, though self-willed, was easily influenced.

They came, and there appeared to be something more than usual on the mind of the young duke; there was a look of eager excitement and, at the same time, of indecision.

No one of the attendants at the castle noticed the unusual look and manner of the duke, except Steward Ruppert and Wido; and in the evening, in the quietude of their own apartment, they spoke of it, but without forming any opinion.

The small bedroom of Wido adjoined a large apartment where Ruppert, as steward of the castle, sat when not on duty, and where he would often remain an hour after Wido was asleep before retiring to his bedroom on the other side.

Wido quickly dropped asleep, as a rule, and was a sound sleeper, as Ruppert knew by experience; but that night Wido lay awake, thinking of the strange manner of the young duke. He also noticed that his father, instead of retiring at his usual hour, was walking to and fro in the adjoining apartment, and he believed that he, too, was wakeful from excitement or anxiety.

It was scarcely past nine o'clock when he heard someone enter and speak in a low tone to his father, and immediately he was alert, and eager to learn who it was, and what the errand was.

"Are you alone, and no one to listen or to interrupt us?" was asked in a low tone, and he recognized the voice as that of Duke Henry.

"Wholly alone, your Highness. Wido is in his room, which is the same with him as being dead. You need not worry on his account nor for any other reason."

"I know your faithfulness to me, Ruppert," said the Duke, "and now I am about to put it to a severe test. As I do not know whether or not you will stand this test, I must make you promise not to divulge what I am about to tell you."

"You may trust me, your Highness; by my soul's salvation, I will be as silent as the grave. You may put full confidence in my word."

"I believe you. Now listen to what I will tell you. You know as well as I that my brother Otto occupies the throne which of right belongs to me. He is, as you know, the eldest son of my father, Henry I, but at the time of Otto's birth he was only Duke of Saxony; when I was born, he was King of Germany; this gives me the right to succeed him as king. It is impossible for me to engage in open battle with him, but in a quicker and easier manner I must have the crown. I do not conceal from myself that my plan is dangerous, and that the ax of the executioner will be my fate if I do not succeed; but I may as well die that way as to have the torment of feeling that I am kept out of my rights. It is Otto or I; and there is no room upon the earth for both."

"Murder! Oh, my prince!" said Ruppert in a low tone of horror. "Surely, you are not in earnest, my Gracious Duke!"

"Never more so; and my true and loyal friends will be my helpers!"

"But oh, remember! King Otto is your brother, and a brother's blood cries to heaven for vengeance. Only a curse, not a blessing, can you expect for such treason against your king and brother."

"This time I am wholly disappointed in you," returned the prince in a tone of displeasure and depression. "But no," he continued in a cheerful, friendly tone; "it is no winder that you do not agree to it, for I have not told you all. You are not to be the one to commit the deed, but only to be leader of the company that is already here. The king is to have a gathering of the great men of his kingdom at the Easter festival at Quedlinburg, and I have been invited. It will not be difficult, in the confusion of the festival, to carry out our plan, and the crown and scepter will be mine. The success of the undertaking will be assured if you are at the helm. An hour after midnight we will set out for Quedlinburg. Now, Ruppert, can I count on you?"

"You know, my prince," replied the steward after a moment of reflection, "that I hate the king and all his adherents, and you know also that I would gladly shed my blood upon the battle-field for you and your cause. I am at all times ready to battle with the sword for you against your enemies and opponents, but a cowardly, dastardly crime, a treacherous assassination, is something in which I dare not take part. Oh, my beloved prince, do not burden your conscience with this terrible sin!"

"I do not wish to urge upon you what I supposed you would be glad to do out of love to me. As I am mistaken in this, there is nothing more to say in that respect. But I hope it is not too much to ask of you to go to Quedlinburg as a protector to me, for it is not unlikely that I may need your strong arm and sword in my undertaking."

"Yes, your Highness may count on me for that duty. I am the right man for protecting you from danger; for such service I am ready, and though I should lose my life. I would shed my last drop of blood for you."

"I thought you would; indeed, I am convinced of it," and after a few more minutes of conversation the duke returned to his guests.

A storm of anxiety and impatience raged in the breast of Wido; he was thrilled with the desire to warn King Otto of his danger. But what could a poor, powerless boy do to accomplish such an undertaking? And should he betray Duke Henry, who would suffer the penalty of death should his treason become known? Betray one who had taken care of his father and himself when they would have perished had he not provided for them in their distress, and had given them a good home at Beleke Castle?

Nevertheless, the king must be warned; but how and by whom? It was a long distance to Quedlinburg, and an hour after midnight Duke Henry and the other conspirators upon swift horses would be on their way; it seemed impossible to warn the king.

Then, as if by inspiration, it seemed to him, the thought of the new friends at Hartrun came into his mind. He would go to them; they were friends of King Otto, and they would know of some way to warn him. He would go to see them this very moment.

Rising quietly, he went stealthily out of his room, secured the key to the wicket-gate, and flew as swiftly as his feet could carry him to Hartrun.

The night was clear, the beams of the full moon lighted field and forest. All nature was at peace; only man was at variance with the Creator of all good.

Risk and Rust joined in a concert of baying when his footsteps were heard, and the call to Hengist and Keringer was answered in the deep voice of their father.

"Who are you?" he asked.

"I am Wido from Castle Beleke. I have something to tell you in secret. Let me in! Every moment is precious!"

Gerhard and his sons appeared immediately, and Wido told them hurriedly what he had overheard.

"The conduct of your father is worthy of all praise. God grant that it is not too late to warn the king! Hengist and

Keringer, saddle your horses quickly; I am sure the horses of the duke and his friends are not more swift than those the king gave you. Risk and Rust shall go with you for protection. Now hurry as much as possible, and God be with you!"

Wido hurried back to Beleke that his absence might not be noticed, and before he reached it, Hengist and Keringer were on their lonely way to Quedlinburg, while their father prayed that they might not be too late, and also for the poor erring one who would slay his brother for a crown.

King Otto had not yet retired for the night when Hengist and Keringer reached the castle of Quedlinburg, but with his guests, in pious remembrance of the blessed festival for which they had met, yet with Christian cheerfulness, was conversing of the peace which ruled in the land at the time, realizing that there was much for which to be grateful, when suddenly the chamberlain entered, pale and excited.

"Your Majesty," he said in a hurried, but suppressed tone, "your brother, Duke Henry, is again bent upon your destruction, and not in open warfare, but by assassination!"

"You surely do not mean murder, the murder of a brother?"

"Yes, your Majesty. Duke Henry and a company of his adherents have bound themselves by oath to put you out of the way during the confusion of the Easter festival, so that the crown may be placed upon his head."

"Impossible of belief! My brother Henry! Who could have invented such a story?"

"It was not invented, it is a terrible truth."

"But from whom did you learn it?"

"From Hengist and Keringer, the boys who saved your life in the forest from the teeth of the bear. In an incredibly short time they have ridden from Hartrun upon the horses you gave them, for the conspirators were to leave Beleke Castle an hour after midnight. They knew they must reach here before them, and give the warning; but the duke and his followers will soon be here."

"God has sent these boys. But in what way did they get knowledge of the plans of the conspirators?"

The chamberlain told the king of Wido's overhearing the conversation between Prince Henry and his father and of his hurrying to Hartrun.

"I believed you when you mentioned Hengist and Keringer, and now I am convinced that the report is entirely correct"; and King Otto's eyes dimmed with tears. "Oh, the shameful treatment of me by that boy! I have tried all I could to satisfy him that I am rightfully occupying the throne. Had not the All-merciful sent His angels to watch over me, there would have been no hindrance in his way to win the crown by the shedding of his brother's blood. For his sake as well as my own I thank God that I have been warned. We have the ablest men of the kingdom with us at this time; I will assemble them immediately to consider with me what plan to take to frustrate this terrible conspiracy."

"You will excuse Hengist and Keringer from appearing in your presence until morning," said the chamberlain; "they were so exhausted from their long ride that I ordered to give them something to eat and told them to go to bed. The horses dropped down when they reached their stalls, from sheer overexertion."

The many guests were called from their apartments, and a conference was held with regard to the celebration of the Easter festival, the whole plan of which was changed, in order to thwart the scheme of the conspirators.

The king received Hengist and Keringer and thanked them heartily while hearing the whole story from them. They also told him that Wido implored him to spare the life of Duke Henry for his terrible treason against his king. Wido asked this out of love and gratitude to Duke Henry, who had saved the life of his father and his own when they, as persecuted Germans, fled from Hungary; and had since given them a good home at Beleke Castle and in every way was a kind and helpful friend.

King Otto invited them to remain for the Easter festival, but they must not allow Duke Henry or his followers to catch sight of them as they might be recognized and suspected of having given the king warning. For the day they could mingle with the crowd unobserved, and as soon as the festival was over, two fresh fine horses would be presented to them by the king that they might return that night to relieve the anxiety of their father.

That morning Duke Henry presented himself at the castle, and the king received him as if no knowledge had come to him of the awful plot against his life; nor did Duke Henry's manner show any evidence of what was in his mind.

The Easter festival was celebrated with great splendor. Otto, upon a beautifully caparisoned horse, led the brilliant procession in kingly attire, the great multitude of young and old greeting him with loyal affection and enthusiasm.

His noble and benign countenance showed no sign of the unrest and anxiety that he endured, knowing that at any moment a deadly poniard might be plunged into his body.

Aside from the crowd stood Ruppert, steward of Beleke Castle, his troubled countenance showing his distress of mind, when he was spoken to by Duke Henry.

"You see that all your anxiety for the king was useless," he said in a low tone. "He certainly has had no warning as you imagine. Do you suppose a sagacious man such as he is would show himself upon the street in this untroubled manner, if he had received a warning? Has he shown one sign of expecting an attack from any quarter? Your anxiety is foolish; you see specters in the clear light of day."

"But your Highness cannot fail to notice that his Majesty is so surrounded and hemmed in by his people that it would be impossible for anyone to force his way to him. He is not willing to let this blessed festival be marred, the people saddened by seeing him looking anxious and distressed. But when the day is past, the mask will be laid aside, and disaster, like a whirlwind will overtake you. Flee from here, your Highness! Go now; in the morning it may be too late."

"Oh, Ruppert, lay aside that wailing! You know that, had we not been delayed on the way to Quedlinburg, the whole business would have been settled by this time. But our whole plan was changed by the accident to the horses. Go now, Ruppert, and look forward to tomorrow."

The following afternoon was the farewell celebration.

A stately parade of horsemen with rich armorial costumes upon splendidly caparisoned horses, the stately form of King Otto in the center, and so compactly surrounded by dukes, counts, and other noblemen that the conspirators had not the least chance to reach him; and all the sad forebodings of Ruppert were renewed in his mind that the king had been warned, and death for treason awaited Duke Henry.

At a place previously agreed upon the parade halted, and a company of the king's men gathered about the conspirators.

"Arrest them," called the strong voice of the Duke of Swabia, and like a lion upon its prey the circle pounced upon Duke Henry and his adherents.

"Surrender! Resistance is useless," called the captors; and in a moment a terrific battle was raging.

"Fly! fly! It is your only chance," cried Ruppert. "Your horse is fleet, break through the king's circle. I will follow you as fast as possible."

Duke Henry took the advice without a moment's delay, and, swift as the bird through the air, master and man passed through a narrow street.

"Let not Duke Henry escape!" called the king. "A rich reward to the captor!"

Six horsemen followed him, but they had reached the open country and were speeding away when they came to a deep trench which their horses refused to spring over; but, goaded by the spurs, they at length made the attempt.

Ruppert's horse cleared it, but that of the duke missed the opposite bank by a few inches and fell on his knees, but his rider was firm in the saddle, and the noble animal, after struggling for a moment for foothold, arose apparently without harm; but while Ruppert's horse sped away like the wind, that of Duke Henry was lamed.

"Lost!" he exclaimed. "Save yourself, Ruppert; it is all up with me."

"Never!" replied the faithful helper; "take my horse," and he flung himself from the saddle.

"It is too much! too much! You will suffer the death penalty; I will not take your horse."

"You must"; and with his giant strength he lifted the duke to the saddle.

"Now away, away! I will follow. I'll plunge into the forest; that is the safest place."

The horses of the pursuers balked at the trench and four of them refused to make the trial of springing over; but the two that followed reached Ruppert. One of them struck him, knocking off his helmet. The blow caused him to fall from his horse, and the men passed on in pursuit of Duke Henry.

6

⚜ Good Friends ⚘

THE DAY AFTER the second appearance of King Otto on the streets of Quedlinburg, closely surrounded by his retinue of noblemen and other faithful adherents, Hengist and Keringer set out upon their return to Castle Hartrun.

They had enjoyed the Easter festival to the limit, were rested from the fatigue of their swift travel the night before Easter, and enjoyed the tranquil journey home. The beautiful experience of the whole affair, especially King Otto's majestic appearance in his royal garb, was something to be remembered.

"It seems strange to me," remarked Hengist, "that six horsemen could not capture Duke Henry, although they followed and searched for him until it grew dark."

"I am wondering what became of Ruppert," replied Keringer. "He was knocked off his horse by one of the horsemen who returned. Search was made for him, but he could not be found, or he would have paid the penalty then and there for treason."

"Listen, brother," said Hengist. "Risk and Rust are howling in the forest; they have found something that is new to them; let us go and see what it is."

They sprang from their horses, tied them to limbs of trees, and followed the sound, which led them to a brook in the forest; and on the shore they saw the body of a man, motionless and apparently lifeless; it was the body of Steward Ruppert.

The hearts of the boys thrilled with compassion for the strong man, helpless, with closed eyes and face deadly pale.

They knelt by him, opened his doublet, and found to their real joy that his heart was beating, though faintly, and eagerly they brought water in their caps from the brook, and sprinkled it upon his face and wrists.

After what seemed a long time, Ruppert gave a feeble sigh, opened his eyes, and after gazing at the brothers for a time, his eyes clouded with anger.

"Well," he exclaimed harshly, "what are you doing here?"

"We are your neighbors at Hartrun."

"Yes, and are adherents of King Otto; I saw you at Quedlinburg, and I was not glad to see you. I suppose you are sent to search for me."

"No, we are on our way home, and coming by the forest we heard the howling of the dogs and followed the sound. We are very glad that we were able to be of some help to you."

"That may be true, but I doubt it."

"But it is true; we bathed your face and wrists with cool water from the brook, and you came to again. Now we will help you on one of the horses and take you to Beleke Castle."

"Why need you trouble yourselves to do that?"

"Because you are not able to walk."

"You will soon see that I can take care of myself; you may betake yourselves to your home."

"It would not be Christian-like at all to leave you here to suffer."

"But I do not wish to have anything to do with you. You are of the king's people; I hate them all."

"After we have taken you to your home, you may think and do as you choose; you can go your way, and we will go ours. But you must not refuse our help. Night is coming on, and you must not lie here alone. Come, we will help you into the saddle."

"It is a shame that I should have met with an accident just at this time, and abominable to be dependent upon you," grumbled Ruppert. "I was fleeing from Quedlinburg with his Highness Duke Henry; his horse sprang over the trench all right, but fell and grew lame. I gave his Grace my horse that he might have a chance to save himself. I was on the lame horse, and the king's men, believing me to be one of the conspirators, knocked me off the horse. I do not know how long I lay there, but when I came to, I walked all that night and the next day. A peasant gave me some bread, which strengthened me so much that I was able to walk on and on, and to my joy I found myself in this blessed forest. I dragged myself to the brook, for I was perishing with fever thirst. Oh, the fine cool water! I drank and drank — and that is all I can remember. The men that struck me thought I was dead. Why I was spared merely to fall into your hands, God only knows."

The boys made no reply, but with all the strength they possessed they helped him on Keringer's horse, who led it, while Hengist walked beside, lending Ruppert the support he needed to keep his seat on the saddle, while leading his own horse.

But for these attentions the steward showed not the least gratitude or friendliness, but seemed to wish he had been left to die by the brook.

His companions, however, paid no attention to his ungrateful behavior, their main desire being to cheer him, and make him feel that they were his friends.

In order to do this, they chatted with each other of their childhood days before coming to Hartrun, of the lake and of Prince Otto, now the king, who had saved Keringer from drowning. Then they spoke of the trials of their parents and of the kidnapping of their little brother Arnulf.

"How old was your little brother when the Hungarians, as you say, made a raid upon your castle and carried him off?" asked Ruppert.

"About a year and a half."

"Have you had no trace of him since?"

"No trace whatever, and our father and mother grieved terribly about it. Mother died when Keringer was five years old. Father often said that he and mother would have been glad to know that little Arnulf was in his grave rather than never to find out what was his fate among the Hungarians."

They were now near Hartrun on their way to Beleke, and they noticed that Ruppert had grown more pale and was trembling, so that it was difficult for Hengist to keep him in the saddle. They had passed the entrance to Hartrun but a little distance when he fell heavily to the ground, unconscious.

Hengist called to his father and the servants, and Ruppert was carried into the castle and laid upon a comfortable bed, which he could not leave for many a day.

Thursday after Easter Wido was in the arbor of the garden at Beleke Castle. He had been to Hartrun Castle, had seen his father, who had suffered and was yet suffering for his treason to King Otto, and had heard from Hengist and Keringer of all that had transpired at Quedlinburg, also that the fate of Duke Henry was still unknown. Yet he could not reproach himself for the part he had taken in warning the king of his danger.

He was pondering over these things when he saw a horseman slowly approaching the secret entrance of the castle, and though it was twilight, he recognized Duke Henry. He went up to him, ready to wait upon him if it were required.

He found the duke standing at a table in the anteroom, upon which he had placed his helmet and sword.

"Oh, miserable man that I am!" he moaned. "Would I not give my life to feel as I did before the terrible thought entered my mind to strive for my brother's crown? Satan blinded me, yes, blinded me!"

Wido stepped in, and the duke turned and held out his trembling hand.

"In the flight your father and I became separated," he said in a subdued tone; "the enemy was in fierce pursuit of me, and I do not know the fate of your father. Oh, Wido, I have burdened my conscience with a terrible crime!"

Wido had in his heart felt keen anger against the one whom he so loved, and who had shown his father and himself so many favors; but seeing his hopeless condition of mind, he could feel nothing but the tenderest pity.

"The enemy lost track of me in the forest," continued the duke, "and will seek me here in my Castle Beleke. No minute while here am I safe. I must resort to flight. But where can I go and not meet trouble, danger, and need — all well-deserved punishment" Oh, that I had never been tempted to do my brother harm! But what has been done cannot be undone, and I must bear it as best I can."

"I can offer your Highness help in only one way," said Wido. "Let me share your flight."

"Oh, Wido, do I really hear right? Would you indeed share my misery?" and a look of great relief came into the duke's pale face. "But remember, I cannot take a horse: my only chance for escape is on foot."

Secretly and silently Duke Henry and Wido left the castle, and set out aimlessly. Only in the humblest dwellings did they dare ask for food, and very often the peasants' wives gave it with words of anger. They considered themselves lucky when they found an empty stable or a lonely haystack where they could obtain shelter for the night; and to save themselves from wild animals, they were compelled to take refuge in the branches of a tree. Often their faces and hands were torn by briars and thorns. Their clothes were worn and torn to rags, so that they were a laughing-stock for the village boys; and more than once they were bitten by dogs.

To add to their distress, the duke sprained his ankle, and walking now caused him great pain.

His despair at times was so keen that he was almost willing to be arrested by the bailiffs of the king, and to have his troubles ended by the ax of the executioner.

An angel of comfort was Wido in these despondent times; he spoke words of cheer, assured him of better days, and did all in his power to comfort him.

Again and again he would speak of the noble, affectionate nature of King Otto, and he comforted the poor misguided Duke Henry with the assurance that no revenge lingered in the heart of the great and good man against his brother, but, instead, mercy and forgiveness. He advised him to go to Quedlinburg, and ask his pardon for the crime he had intended to commit.

At first this seemed a terrible thought to Duke Henry, but as Wido continued to present it, his objections grew fainter, and he began to consider it in the same light as his young friend and companion.

"You are right," he said one day after a conversation with Wido, and when his need had reached the highest point; "I will put myself entirely in the hands of my brother, whom I treated so shamefully. I have sinned grievously against him, but maybe his love and compassion will be greater than my sin. What I have done against him fills me with remorse; but it has led me to repentance. If Otto forgives me, I will be his faithful friend unto death. Love for him and faithfulness shall be my watchword."

Now that Duke Henry had decided to go to his brother, they changed their course, and with weary feet went towards Quedlinburg. Completely exhausted and sad of heart they reached it. With bare feet and as a repentant sinner Duke Henry threw himself upon his knees at the feet of the king.

"Forgive me, Otto! Never again will I cause you sorrow or grief."

"You have indeed caused me much suffering," replied the king. "If there were no love and pity in my heart for you, I would give you up this minute to suffer the full penalty of the law. But I do believe you are sincere in your love for me, and I believe in your repentance. I freely and fully forgive you, and will spare your head from the ax of the executioner by fully forgiving you."

Under a strong guard King Otto sent him to the imperial palace at Ingelheim. Wido, however, was not sentenced to accompany him, but returned to his home anxious to see his father.

Duke Henry's eyes were dim with tears when he bade the faithful friend farewell. Wido, while feeling glad to know that the wanderings of the one he so loved were past, was not entirely free from worry with regard to him.

In the meantime Ruppert's life had hung in the balance, though under the faithful care of the father and sons at Hartrun. At times he had lain unconscious, and again he had been delirious with fever.

Day and night his good Samaritans were at his bedside. Cold bandages were laid upon his forehead, his lips were moistened with cold water, and all that might distress him in regard to Duke Henry was kept from him. But notwithstanding all their devoted care of him, he did not seem to be on the road to recovery. Sometimes he realized their kindness to him, and grieved that he had not the strength to tell them of his sincere gratitude and of his regret that he had hated them because they were adherents of King Otto.

Gerhard had noticed for some time that the mind of the invalid was troubled, and hoped he would speak of it, without making any effort, however, to bring it about.

But one evening, when the two were by themselves, Ruppert spoke.

"Come a little nearer to me, Gerhard von Stein," he said feebly. "I have for several days been wishing to speak of something that lies heavy upon my heart. I think it has been a long time since I was brought into this room, and had I been a dear friend, you and your sons could have done no more for me than you have done. I had never given you a friendly word, but you have returned good for evil. It seemed unbearable to me to be compelled to accept assistance from your sons when I lay helpless by the brook in the forest. It was God's will that I should be brought to Hartrun Castle.

"The kindness and tenderness that you have daily and hourly shown me has softened my heart. The hate fostered in it has disappeared like dew in the sun. The hate I harbored against you was only owing to your being adherents of King Otto, when I knew that my Duke Henry should have been king. But that feeling of hate is gone from my heart. Can you forgive me, Gerhard von Stein?"

"I forgave you long ago," was the answer which came from the bottom of the heart. "We all knew that you had a kind heart, and that it was your loyalty to Duke Henry, who had befriended you when you so needed help, that made you look upon us as his enemies."

"I do thank you for these words. And now I wish to tell you, as I said, of something that has been burdening my heart. You believe Wido to be my son, but" — he could say no more; a deadly paleness spread over his features, and he grew faint and helpless.

Gerhard applied restoratives and after a little while Ruppert revived, but did not seem inclined to renew the conversation, while his host naturally wished to hear more.

"You were speaking of Wido," he said. "If you feel equal to it, I would be glad to hear what you wished to tell me." "I cannot call to memory what it was that I intended telling you. Oh, yes, now I know. But I feel too weak now; I will tell you all as soon as I will be able to do so."

When Wido reached home and found that his father was at Hartrun, he hurried there, and was rejoiced to find him so improved that a few days later they returned to Beleke Castle.

Time passed on, and peace reigned between the two castles Hartrun and Beleke; happy, contented life in the country.

It was now the joyous Christmas time of 941, and winter ruled in its most rigorous form. Mountains, meadows, and the bridges over the Rhine and other rivers wore thick mantles of snow, and the whole face of Nature was shadowed by a gray sky, which foreboded a deeper covering of the white mantle.

Weeks had passed since Duke Henry had become a prisoner of the imperial palace at Ingelheim, weeks which seemed years.

He was surrounded by every comfort and privilege, and had no cause to complain of anything except his loss of liberty.

His change from the terrible dread of arrest by the king's bailiffs, he felt, should have given him serene content; instead, he was full of anxiety and unrest, his treason against the king had robbed him of all peace.

Shame and regret were ever present with him, and robbed him of sleep. His mother, Queen Matilda, had interceded for him with the king. Henry had always been her favorite son, and he was confident for a time that her pleadings would avail, and that he would be set free; but as yet he was a prisoner.

There was a young chaplain in the imperial palace who took a deep interest in the royal prisoner; but for a time his cheering words struck no responsive chord in the heart of the young duke.

"If my brother does not pardon me," he said to the chaplain two days before Christmas, "I do not know how I am to endure life. No one but he has the power to free me, and he can do this only by a free pardon."

"I do not believe that King Otto could refuse it if he would see you, and you would ask it in person. He will be in Frankfort to celebrate the Christmas festival, and it would he a good opportunity for you to see him. I will accompany you to Frankfort if you wish."

Duke Henry gladly accepted the chaplain's offer, and the latter selected three of the attendants as guides and protectors, and secretly and silently they left the castle that night, and started on their long walk, the young duke in the garb of a penitent.

The next day they rested in a deserted hut in a forest, and that night took up their journey again, reaching Frankfort in the morning just as the bells were ringing the Christmas matins.

"Your Highness will gather strength and courage in listening to the bells proclaiming peace on earth and good will to men," said the chaplain cheerfully.

"Yes, they are; and oh, how loving and forgiving they sound to me! My brother Otto never fails to attend matins in the church; he will be here, and I shall see him. Surely in this holy place he will not turn from me; he will listen to my petition."

In the dimness of the pillared, arched entrance stood Duke Henry; he had removed his foot-covering, and with bare feet, as a penitent, he waited for the king.

He had not long to wait. Soon the noble, majestic form of his brother Otto was seen to enter the portal. From behind one of the pillars the penitent came quickly forward, and threw himself at his feet, his bowed head almost touching the floor.

Deep sobs convulsed his frame, and no words came from his pale lips.

King Otto was deeply touched, and tears of pity and brotherly love filled his eyes as he looked from his height to the prostrate man.

"Is it indeed Henry?" he asked in a kind tone, and he stretched forth his hand to raise him from the marble floor of the cathedral.

"I am not worthy to look upon your face, but will lie here until you grant me forgiveness and pardon for the sake of the risen Christ, whom you so honor, pardon for your sinning, but truly repentant brother!"

King Otto's eyes were dim with tears, and for a moment he was silent. "This day," he said, "the Son of God came upon earth, and by His life and death won forgiveness for the sins of men. He should be an example for me. *On earth peace, good will to men,* sang the angels, and there should be peace between my brother and me. I will not only pardon your sin against me, but it shall he as though it had never been committed."

Saying this, King Otto raised his brother from the floor, and pressed him to his heart.

From that hour Duke Henry was a faithful friend of his noble-hearted brother, and King Otto never had reason to regret that he had brought peace to his repentant kinsman on that blessed Christmas morning.

He gave back to him the Grand Duchy of Bavaria, which he had forfeited, and all else of which his treason had deprived him. As Duke of Bavaria Henry did the kingdom an inestimable service, for in 949 the Hungarians again broke into Germany, first swarming over Bavaria. But this time Duke Henry was victorious; as no one had done before, he vanquished the Hungarians and secured from the robbers all the treasures they had taken from the Germans.

Duke Henry did not keep it a secret that his intended assassination of the king was frustrated by Wido, Hengist, and Keringer, and was deeply grateful to them for saving him from the frightful deed. He felt that he never could repay them.

He was deeply anxious to take Wido to Bavaria, that he might be always near him, but to this Ruppert would not give consent. "Your Highness," he said, "without him I would not care to live; I know it is selfish in me, and I am standing in the boy's way to progress; but he is my only treasure in life; he is my comfort."

Thus it was that Wido remained at Beleke, and the greatest friendship existed between him and Hengist and Keringer.

7

❧ A Future Queen ❧

IN ONE OF THE WALLED CITIES of Burgundy was a fine castle, one of the residences of the ruler of that kingdom, and where he, the queen, and their young daughter Adelheid, with many attendants and servants, lived at times during each year.

Not only was the castle an attractive home, but the surroundings were all that could be desired, for nature and art had combined to beautify them.

Adjoining the large garden with its myriads of flowers and shrubs was a forest belonging to the estate. One summer afternoon, in the year 945, Adelheid, wishing a change from the garden, unlocked the small gate leading into the forest, and for the first time in her fourteen years of life viewed the new and varied beauties about her.

Under the shadows of the great trees she gathered wild flowers, the rays of sunlight which gleamed between the branches lighting her beautiful blond hair, bright eyes, and fair, innocent, childlike face.

After a time her attention was attracted by a squirrel that ran up the trunk of a tree and sprang lightly from limb to limb; and when it disappeared, she returned to the bank which overlooked a brook running between the rocks, and sat down to listen to its gentle murmur.

The moss upon the bank was soft and made a pleasant place to rest, with a gentle elevation, which served as a pillow, and without being conscious of it, she fell asleep.

There was no sound to disturb her, the place was safe

from intruders, and there was no fear in her mind of anything that would harm to cause her to keep awake. But between the rocks glided a viper; it crept up the bank upon which lay the sleeping girl, and noiselessly coiled up upon her breast.

In the meantime a girl of nearly the age of Adelheid had passed through the park on the way from the city to her home, and, seeing the gate open that led to the forest, she concluded to shorten her way by passing through.

Her quick glance saw the danger to the sleeping girl. Her face paled; however, she did not lose her presence of mind, but, stepping quietly to some brushwood lying near, she selected a straight, strong stick, slipped it under the sleeping serpent, and threw it with force against a rock. It was stunned and unable for a moment to move, and the girl, with quick strokes of the stick, killed it.

Adelheid was awakened by the blows, and gazed in surprise at the girl beside her.

"Who are you?" she asked. "Did I dream that I heard someone striking with a stick?"

"No, you did not dream; I will show you," and she brought the viper to her on the rod, explained her presence in the forest, and expressed her joy at having come in time to kill the reptile.

"It might have bitten both of us," said Adelheid with a shudder. "Come, let us thank the dear Father in heaven for sparing our lives," and kneeling down by the bank, she gave thanks. Then the two sat on the bank to talk over the strange meeting.

"Will you tell me your name?" asked Adelheid.

"Yes; it is Hedwig, and my father was a water-toll collector; the place was given him by our good king. We lived in a little house on the shore, and were so happy, we four; but my mother died last year, and my father was killed by a bear only a few weeks ago." Tears filled her blue eyes at the remembrance.

"Did you always live in Burgundy?"

"Yes; but my father and mother were Germans; and my mother lived in a count's family here in Burgundy as ladies' companion. My father was named Conrad, and when the king gave him the place, and the house to live in, he and my mother were married."

"Are you entirely alone in the house?"

"I will be, for my brother Hildeward went this morning to Germany to see if any of our parents' relatives will give me a home if I do not get one here. We know that there is a brother of my father, named Gerhard von Stein, and a brother of my mother, named Gozbert, who is in the service of King Otto as forester and huntsman. I hope he will get back safely."

"What will you do now that he is away?"

"I will try to get work; I am strong and love to work."

"Come and see my mother," said Adelheid eagerly; "she will care for you, and will be glad to see you because you saved me from the viper."

"Is your home far from here?" asked Hedwig, in whose breast the invitation had raised a hope.

"No, it is in that castle with a high tower."

"There?" exclaimed Hedwig in astonishment. "Is your father a rich man?"

"I do not know; but he is king of Burgundy."

"Then you are a princess!" and the girl's face showed such surprise and admiration that Adelheid laughed gleefully.

"Certainly! You must have seen me some time when you passed through the park."

"No; and I never thought of you being a princess because you are here alone. Do not think ill of me for talking to you as if you were a poor girl like me."

"You foolish girl! If you only knew how glad I am to be with someone who talks to me as she would to other girls."

"Then you will not think me too bold if I ask you a question?"

"No; tell me exactly what you wish, and I will answer if I can."

"Does your mother know that you are out in this forest alone?"

"No; and it is no wonder that you think it strange," and her sweet face flushed; "I will tell you how it was.

"I am allowed to be by myself in the garden every afternoon. When I have learned all my lessons in the morning, I am free for two hours. The garden, as you know, is surrounded by a high wall. It is a lovely place, but I was tired of it, and longed to see the forest, where there are so many new things. As you see, I am near the postern gate, which leads to the garden, and would hear the first call; but I did not know there were vipers here. Now come with me and see my mother."

They clasped hands, ran through the postern gate, locked it, and went up the steps of the castle and to the apartment where Adelheid knew she would find her mother.

"Mother, this is Hedwig; she has neither father nor mother, and her brother has gone to Germany, and she will be alone in the house. Please let her come to live with us." The queen was well pleased with the modest appearance of the girl, and after some conversation found her to be intelligent and companionable, and she believed they would not be mistaken in giving her a home.

Nor were they mistaken, as years of companionship and helpfulness proved. Lovely in disposition, kind in her ways, never forgetting the difference of their social position, she was at all times a true and faithful, but humble friend.

Several weeks after Hedwig had found a good home in the castle, a boy of about sixteen years, handsome of face and straight of form, was walking through a forest near Merseburg in Germany. Upon his dark, curly hair rested a fur cap, in which was an eagle's feather, and over his shoulder was slung a cross-bow, a quiver of arrows, and a bugle. In his right hand was a hunting-spear, and in his belt a bright knife.

In appearance and manner he bore such a resemblance to Wido that they would have been taken for brothers.

Upon reaching the edge of the forest, he saw the form of an elderly man of almost giant size, with broad shoulders, and gray hair and beard. In his hands was a bow from which an arrow had evidently been sent at a wild animal of some kind.

The boy secreted himself, and a moment later a roe came in view looking about it as if scenting danger. It had not lowered its head when an arrow of the huntsman whistled through the air, but missed its aim. The roe sprang away, coming directly in view of the traveler, who had taken his bow from his shoulder, fitted it with an arrow, and took aim. The roe made a leap into the air, and then fell to the ground; the arrow had done its work.

The gray-bearded hunter stepped from the tall bushes and came to look at the roe.

"Ruppert — are you really Ruppert, or do my eyes deceive me?" exclaimed the boy.

"What do you mean? I am not Ruppert."

"You are the living image of a man I know."

"I have a twin brother, and his name is Ruppert, but he lives in Saxony, miles and miles from here. I would like to know who you are."

"Hildeward is my name. I came from Burgundy, and see," he continued as he stooped down to the roe, "my arrow struck exactly where it was aimed."

"It did," responded the hunter. "How long have you been on your travels?"

"About two weeks; I did not come directly here, but stopped for three days on the Lippe River, for there I became acquainted with your brother Ruppert and his son Wido. I met them in the forest, where they were hunting, and was their guest for three days at Beleke Castle. You may well say that Ruppert is your brother; for such a resemblance I could not believe possible; his face, form, voice, and manner are exactly yours."

"For years we have not been as brothers, but enemies. Some years ago Ruppert left Hungary for Germany. It was at the time the Hungarians fought King Henry I, father of King Otto, in 933. In the battle Ruppert was struck on the head, and badly injured. By God's mercy, Henry, King Otto's younger brother, who was hunting, found him; and the noble son of a noble king took care of him and his miserable family, and helped them on their way to Saxony.

"Of course, Ruppert was deeply grateful, and by right should be; but he need not, through good and evil, stay on his side as he has always done. You must have heard that this same Duke Henry has tried to take his brother's life, but through even this evil against King Otto, Ruppert has stood heart and soul with Duke Henry.

"As, naturally, I stood by King Otto, you may well believe that in these perilous times I will not speak well of my brother. But that is all in the past. Henry asked pardon of the king, it was granted, and now Ruppert is no longer an antagonist of King Otto."

"Yes; Ruppert kept nothing of this from me," remarked Hildeward; "he was truly friendly, and we were sorry to part."

"Now listen, boy," said the hunter, who had been eying the roe; "you appear to be a good shot; I believe the arrow went to the roe's heart. Was its shoulder your aim?"

"Your question vexes me," laughed Hildeward. "My arrow scarcely ever errs from the point I wish it to make; I aimed for the heart."

"Now, boy, I do not wish to offend you, but you must have had a good instructor to make you so adept."

"It was my father; he was known far and near for his skill in the use of weapons; yet he was not a hunter, but a gatherer of water-tolls."

"I believe you; and I cannot understand how I failed to hit that roe; it has been many years since I missed my aim. The eye of a deer is not too small a target for my arrow."

"I am sure of that, and the most skillful of hunters cannot say that they never miss their aim."

"I am heartily glad that your arrow brought down the roe. Early tomorrow morning a fine roast of it will be in the kitchen of the king's castle at Merseberg. King Otto and his son Ludolph are there now, and no one loves a roast of young deer better than King Otto, and I do thank you for your sure aim."

"Does King Otto ever hunt in this forest?"

"Yes, when his Majesty sojourns at Merseburg. He loves to hunt in the German forests."

"I hope I may have a chance to see your king."

"That will be easily done. It is understood that you are to stay with me in my hunter's cabin as long as you will, for I cannot deny that I am well pleased with you. Come now; it is time for supper. The jay is sounding its evening call, which means that night is not far off."

"I heartily thank you for your invitation, but as yet I do not know who it is that is so kind as to invite me." "Have I not told you that I am a hunter?" laughed his new friend as they started out. "And yet I was not always a hunter. I was a soldier and served as a forester to King Henry, the father of King Otto, when there were times of peace. Truly, when a feud was on hand, my soldier blood was up; I could not remain in the forest, but took part in all the battles."

"But you have not told me your name. How will I know you are my uncle unless I know your name?"

"Your uncle? Gozbert is my name; but that does not make me your uncle."

"Yes, it does. Did you not have a sister named Hadamoth?"

"Yes, certainly; but I have not heard of her for a long-time. Do you bring news of her?"

"Your sister Hadamoth was my mother; she died half a year ago."

"You, the son of my sister Hadamoth?" exclaimed the hunter joyously as he clasped the hand of Hildeward. "Oh, boy, I never expected such happiness!"

"And to think that I was with Ruppert and Wido three days, and they did not mention that they were uncle and cousin to me. My mother often spoke to me of her brother Gozbert, but I did not know she had a brother Ruppert. Nor did Wido tell me that it was my uncle Gerhard von Stein that owned that fine estate Hartrun.

"I wish I had come to see you first, then I would have known that my uncle Gerhard von Stein had left the old fortress that my father had spoken of, and where I expected to visit him.

"How did he get that splendid property, uncle?"

"It was given to him by King Otto for some service Gerhard had done him. All the world spoke of the splendid gift, and in this way it came to my ears. But what I wish to ask of you is: How was it that your father left the homeland, and how did he make the acquaintance of my sister Hadamoth?" It was a surprise to me that she married Conrad von Stein, the brother of a knight."

"I have never heard his reason for leaving the old homestead. All I know is that he took service in the family of a count, and there became acquainted with my mother. Through the influence of that nobleman he got the position of collector of water-tolls.

"We lived very happily in our small house on the shore. Now my sister Hedwig is alone, but we have kind neighbors there, and they will take care of her until I return."

8

✄ A Change of Homes ✄

TWILIGHT REIGNED in the forest when Gozbert and his nephew reached their destination, the small cabin with two rooms. It was built of logs, filled in with earth and lime, and the floor was sanded.

The roof was made of poles covered with reeds and rushes, which kept out snow and rain, and the only window in the hut was covered with parchment, which allowed a dim light to stream into the hut.

The door was so low that both men had to stoop to enter, and the room seemed almost bare of furniture, only a rough table and blocks of wood for seats, and the bedroom adjoining was quite as simple in its appointments.

The roe had been carried to the cabin on the shoulder of Gozbert, and it was but short work for the two to provide from it steaks for supper, which Gozbert broiled over the open fire in the huge fireplace, and which, with brown bread, made a supper that was entirely satisfactory. When finished, Hildeward put the few dishes and pans back on the shelf, and they took seats under the spreading branches of a great oak that shaded a spring gushing forth clear, cold water.

"I hope you will stay with me, Hildeward," said his uncle; "it would be the greatest joy of my heart. I have long wished for a helper, and one is really needed for the forest and in the hunt, and King Otto has more than once spoken of the need. Now promise me that you will stay."

"It seems hardly fair to you not to promise, uncle,"

replied the young man. "I would have no employment in my old home, while it will be no trouble to Hedwig to secure a place in a home. Her neighbors will help her, for they love her almost as they do their own children."

For some time uncle and nephew conversed in the cool, fragrant place on the edge of the forest, and then retired to their place of rest. Bear-skins with light covering was all that was required, and they slept the sleep that active outdoor life gives.

At daylight they were awakened by a rapping at the door with a stick, the caller being on horseback.

"Wake up, Gozbert," said a voice he recognized as one of the huntsmen. "The king, Prince Ludolph, and several gentlemen of the court are out upon a hunt of wild boars. A whole herd has broken through the mountain enclosure, and are roaming about the forest. We are to wait for the king at the usual place. Hurry out, so that you won't keep us waiting."

Uncle and nephew sprang to their feet, and in a few minutes were out upon their way, weapons in hand.

"Is not Prince Ludolph too young for such a dangerous hunt?" asked Hildeward as they hurried along.

"You need not imagine the young prince to be a weakling; he is as tall as you, and for two or three years has joined in the hunt with his father. There is no better training for young men than the hunt. Every nobleman and knight knows that the hunt trains their sons for war. A king, above all others, should know this. It is never too early for a young man to hunt wild animals. He must learn all the rules of the hunt, and a prince especially must know that the wild animals of the forest must not gain the mastery. Let him join in the hunt with spear and bow and attack the wild and, sometimes, ferocious animals, and he will learn as much as if fighting men."

"Do you suppose the king expects a great hunt to-day?"

"No; for if he did, preparations would have been made yesterday by bringing many good hunters together, food would be provided, and tents for shelter for the night. Then, if ladies were to be in the company, many arrangements for their comfort would have to be made."

King Otto and his company had not arrived when they reached the appointed place, but they heard hunting-horns, and soon the whole party came in sight.

Besides King Otto and Prince Ludolph there were twenty other horsemen, with all the weapons of the hunt and with hunting-horns of silver or costly ivory. By them, signals were given, also directions, instructions, or, perhaps, reprimands.

King Otto's quick eye soon took notice of Hildeward.

His stately form and handsome face pleased him well, and he wondered who he might be.

"Ha, old man! At last you have come across a helper that is of some account," he said. "You have been in the service of King Henry for many years, and it is time for you to have someone to depend upon. Who is he?"

The old hunter took keen pleasure in telling the king of the unexpected coming of his nephew, and of his wish to keep him. "He is a first cousin of Hengist and Keringer von Stein," he added by way of explanation.

Hildeward was charmed with the appearance of the king and his son Ludolph. The latter rode upon a spirited horse, that pranced and stamped, eager for the hunt; but the prince held him with a firm, though gentle hand.

He was watching the king as he conversed with Gozbert, and then rode up to Hildeward.

"I could tell that you are a cousin of the von Stein boys because you look so much like Hengist. In what way are you related?"

"Their father, Gerhard von Stein, and my father, Conrad von Stein, were brothers."

"I wish you would stay at my side during the hunt, if possible," said the prince. "Our horses must be left with the grooms when we follow the wild animals through the thickets and among trees."

Soon the forest echoed with the sound of horns and the calls of the hunters, and a little later the dark forms of the wild boars were seen trying to escape.

The prince and Hildeward were together, when they heard the rustling of dry twigs and leaves in the bushes, and out rushed one of the largest of the animals, evidently wounded.

The prince sprang aside to avoid collision, when the hunter who had wounded it ran with a long spear to send the animal to the ground, but it turned suddenly, the spear missed its mark, and the tusks of the enraged animal were run into one of the limbs of the prostrate man.

Ludolph sprang to his rescue with his spear, but before he could use it, he was thrown to the ground, and his life hung by a thread. However, before the teeth of the animal could reach his throat, a spear thrown by Hildeward pierced it through the heart.

The prince, dazed from the suddenness of the attack and from fright, could scarcely realize that he was not injured, and stretched out his arms to his deliverer.

"You saved my life," he said, pale and trembling from emotion. "This shall never be forgotten."

"From my heart I thank God that He gave me an opportunity to be of service to you. But we must look after the poor man who did his best to save you."

The two knelt beside the huntsman and examined his wounds. They found that, while deep, they were not dangerous. They bound them up as well as they could, and the prince called for help and had a litter made, so that he might be carried to a safe place.

The king soon heard of the affair, and quickly coming to the spot, he embraced his son with the deepest emotion.

"The Almighty has indeed been wonderfully kind to us; and how wonderful it is that two members of a family have been saved from death, and by four members of another family, and these in different parts of the country, I from the teeth and claws of a bear, you from the tusks and teeth of this ferocious animal that lies dead before us.

"I was saved from assassination by three young men of the same family, and you, my son, from a terrible death by another member of that family. Now, my young friend," he added, turning to Hildeward, "tell me of what help I can be

to you, and do not fear that you are asking too much. I and
my family owe much to you."

"Father," said Prince Ludolph, "ask him to come and live
in the castle with us. I would love to have him for a dear
companion."

"You have made a good proposition. I shall be glad if the
young man will accept. How is it, my young friend, will you
agree to my son's request?"

"Pardon me, your Majesty, but I must first ask my uncle
Gozbert's consent. He asked me last evening at his cabin to
remain with him, and I promised to do so. I must agree to
what be says."

"Just what I would expect of you. Now the question rests
with your uncle, and we will do as he desires in the matter."

A look of keen disappointment stole over the features
of Gozbert when he was told of the request of Ludolph,
but, considering the advantage to his nephew, he made no
protests

"It is like taking a piece out of my heart to give him up,"
he said. "It would be a great pleasure to me to have him in
my home, but I bow to the will of my king; I give him up to
you."

"Your nephew shall not be entirely taken from you; as
often as you wish and he desires he may be with you in your
home in the forest."

"Will I always be welcome to come, uncle?" asked Hildeward. "I enjoyed my short visit with you, and would like
to come again."

"You cannot come too often; you will only be too welcome."

Hildeward now had an enviable home in the castle at
Merseburg; but he equally loved the old cabin in the forest,
and his visits there were the bright spots in the life of his
uncle Gozbert.

As time passed on, the king and his court sojourned
at different castles in his kingdom, and Hildeward always
accompanied his beloved friend Ludolph; but whenever
within reaching distance of the cabin in the Merseburg forest, he never failed to visit it.

9

❧ A Family Council ❧

TWO YEARS HAD PASSED since Hedwig had saved Princess Adelheid from the teeth of the viper, and much had transpired in those two years.

Scarcely beyond childhood, the beautiful and lovable princess had become, in the year 947, the wife of the nineteen-year-old King Lothair of Italy.

Lothair was the son of King Hugas, and had been declared king during the lifetime of his father.

After the splendid wedding festival had been celebrated, Adelheid accompanied her husband to her new home in Italy. Hedwig was not separated from her, but was still her beloved companion, and the love and loyalty of the girl to the young queen was unbounded.

It would have been difficult to have found a happier wedded pair than Lothair and Adelheid. It could not be otherwise, for both were noble of heart and pious, and it was a marriage from love and appreciation of each other.

Adelheid's beauty was spoken of in all lands; and not only her beauty, but her amiability and charm of manner and sweet simplicity of character.

Lothair also had a noble character and in appearance he was kingly. He was tall and he had the dark eyes and hair of his countrymen; and his kindness and consideration for every one made him greatly beloved and honored.

But scarcely three years of this beautiful life had been passed, when clouds and darkness caused by others took the place of happiness.

In the year 950, the young king and queen, who had resided three years in Pavia, changed their place of residence to Turin.

That Lothair had some good reason for departing from the custom of former rulers was known to Adelheid, but as he did not mention the reason, she made no inquiry. She felt in her heart, however, that it was something that caused him anxiety. Often he appeared in deep thought or in seeming perplexity, and sometimes his sad eyes rested upon his loved and lovely wife with deep sadness.

In November of that year he took his customary evening walk, accompanied by a servant, the walk extending to his hunting-lodge in the forest. He returned with an anxious expression upon his pale features, and Queen Adelheid could no longer refrain from giving expression to her anxiety and sympathy.

"Tell me, Lothair, what it is that troubles you, and has taken all joy out of your heart and mine. It distresses me that I cannot share your trouble."

The king glanced upon her with a look of the tenderest affection, and seemed about to tell her; he hesitated, however, and seemed to consider, and the moment passed.

"I cannot be happy seeing that something troubles you; I am sure that your burden would be lightened by sharing it with a true and faithful friend."

"I believe it is unjust to you to keep it from you," he replied sadly. "Come, my Adelheid, and sit by me, and I will tell you my secret trouble. It is because of Count Berengarius, of whom you have often heard. As you know, his wife Willa is one of our House, for she and I are brother's children. In consequence of this relationship Berengarius, through the influence of Willa, gave much trouble to my father, King Hugas, and in various ways has sought to do many things to my disadvantage.

"Berengarius is cunning, artful, avaricious, and covetous, and would halt at no means to secure his aim to displace me and put himself upon the throne.

"His wife is tyrannical and longs for power. Woe to anyone who incurs her hatred; and there is no one whom she and Berengarius hate as they hate me, and through me they hate you; and both are vindictive and revengeful."

"We have never done harm to them in any way; why do they hate us?"

"To make it clear to you, I must go back to the year 940, when there was disagreement between my father and Berengarius in regard to the crown, and Berengarius, being the weaker, had to take to flight. He took refuge first to Herman, Duke of Swabia, and later to King Otto of Germany; and when my father demanded him of this proud king, his answer was, 'Far be it from me to betray one to whom I have given protection.'

"In a year Berengarius returned of his own free will to Italy, with the vain hope that he could overpower my father with weapons in the hands of brave soldiers. By skillful management he had made many of the great of the kingdom traitors to my father, and on account of their treason and disloyalty they had to resort to flight.

"I, though young, was sent to Milan to gather the great people of the realm to put the crown of the kingdom upon my head. I found no opposition and was called to the throne. All this was against the wishes of Berengarius, for he was expecting the crown for himself, and very soon after, my father died very suddenly. Since then Berengarius has the appearance of being a well-meaning adviser and defender of me and mine, but I know the craftiness and treachery of himself and his wife. They want the crown; I am standing in their way, and they would put me out of that way without scruple."

"Oh, you frighten me!" exclaimed Adelheid, turning very pale, while Lothair's face was almost ghastly. "You do not look well; tell me, are you ailing?"

"Yes, I am not feeling well; I hope it will pass over. I feel faint. I will go and lie down. Do not feel anxious, Adelheid; if God wills, I will be better in the morning."

The young queen spent the night in watching, Hedwig beside her, both hoping for the best. Perfect silence reigned in the palace, and as Hedwig passed two servants in the corridor, she heard one of them whisper, "I fear he is poisoned."

When she returned to the sick-room, she told the queen what she had heard, and the horrified listener could with difficulty repress a scream, for that terrible thought had never entered her mind. She felt that she must tell Lothair what had been said, and he listened without surprise.

"Yes, I believe the man is right," he said; "the enemies' cunning has outmastered my caution. I knew when I first felt ill that poison had been given me, and I also know how it was done. I kept it a secret from you, hoping all the time that the physician's skill could counteract it. All means have been used without your knowledge, knowing your distress of mind should you be told of it. But now it is all in vain, and I feel that you should be told; the way to the throne will soon be open."

Queen Adelheid wrung her hands and wept and moaned; and Hedwig's heart ached for them as she silently wept.

"Listen, my beloved Adelheid," said Lothair, "and I will tell you how this affliction came upon me. I was on my way home from my visit to the hunting-lodge and had reached the edge of the forest, and halted to view the fine landscape spread before me from the bank of the brook. I seldom ride or walk there that I do not halt, and feel refreshed by the lovely scene. I alighted from my horse, for a neat-looking little girl had come by with a basket of plums, fine and fresh, of the kind I like, and without a thought of danger I selected some and gave her a gold piece for them. They were fully ripe and rich in flavor, and being thirsty, I ate all that I had selected.

"When I finished, and was about to mount my horse, I asked the child if the plums had grown in her father's garden. She said, 'No,' but a strange gentleman had given the little basketful to her, and told her that a distinguished knight would pass that way, and that he would buy them and pay her richly.

"Like a flash of lightning," continued the king, "it came to me that the plums were poisoned, and I wondered at my lack of thought in buying them. But a ray of hope came with the thought that many of my friends knew of my fondness for the fruit, and had sent them. Another comfort was that no one would give the child the poisoned fruit without warning her not to eat them. But even with this in mind, I threw all that were left into the brook. For some time I did not feel the effects of eating the fruit; then I began to feel faint, and it was only with some effort that I could collect my thoughts. But I kept it from you. Now, however, I feel that it is better to tell you that you may beware of Berengarius and Willa."

Lothair's voice grew very weak before he finished, and later he grew unconscious, and before morning he passed away.

The young queen was overcome with grief. Hedwig was her comfort in the bitter trial and loss she had sustained.

The body of the young king lay in state for several days that the people might see the one they had so esteemed. Then it was placed in an iron-bound casket and taken to Milan.

In the beginning of April of the following year Adelheid with her friend Hedwig and her faithful servants returned to Pavia, a step which she had great cause to regret, for in a palace at Pavia Count Berengarius and his wife Willa were watching the trend of events.

One evening the count was walking restlessly to and fro in one of the apartments of the castle. He would have been handsome were it not for a wavering, dissatisfied look in his eyes and a morose expression about his mouth. Evidently he was expecting someone, for he frequently halted to listen.

At length footsteps were heard in the corridor, and his wife entered, accompanied by their young son Adelbert.

Both were richly dressed, and strongly resembled each other, the same sinister expression making their countenances anything but agreeable.

"I have waited for at least half an hour for you, Willa," said Berengarius in a harsh, complaining tone, "for I have an important and agreeable message to give you."

"Important and agreeable!" she exclaimed, the light of hope causing her black eyes to glisten. "Nothing would give me greater pleasure next to having heard of the death of

Lothair than that our way is now open to the throne after
so much delay. Is your news in that line?"

"You have guessed it. The business is now on the way to
secure the crown of Italy for myself and Adelbert."

"Oh, the delight of knowing this!" exclaimed Willa, a
flush of joy rising to her face. "What other steps have been
taken in that direction?"

"Yesterday there was a gathering here in Pavia of the
representative men of the kingdom, and I made it plain to
them that there were no heads that could justly wear the
crown of Italy but Adelbert's and mine. They saw the truth
of this, and chose us as kings of Italy."

"Oh, what a triumph!" exclaimed his wife, almost beside
herself with joy. "What a weight is lifted from my heart! The
uncertainty has been so wearing upon us, has been so hard
to bear. Now at last the aim long striven for is reached. At
last you came to believe in my view of the case as to the best
and quickest way to the throne of Italy. Lothair — but no!
the dead cannot speak! Come, Adelbert, your mother must
be first to embrace the young king of Italy, and to rejoice
that a king's crown is upon your head."

"Do not rejoice too soon, Willa," advised Berengarius,
and his forehead was darkened by some oppressive thought.
"To wear the crown pleases me well, and is something over
which one may rejoice, but as yet we do not know but someone will rise up and strive against us for it."

"Oh, it always suits you to cast shadows; with you we
must always hear raven-croaks. My motto is *death and destruction to whoever stands in our way.* With this for a guide,
what have we to fear?"

"But let us handle this important question in a sensible
manner. Not all the obstructions are yet put aside, and it
is possible that some may rise that we do not expect. Our
sudden good fortune will, no doubt, make enemies. With
the death of Lothair one great obstacle fell out of the way;
but remember that Adelheid is yet living. She considers herself, and not without reason, the rightful heir to the throne
in place of her departed husband, and, no doubt, there are
many in the kingdom who will be loyal to the beloved and

wonderfully beautiful young queen; and should she reach out her hand for the crown, our position will be far from certain."

"Then we must see that she does not make a demand for it by placing her in new circumstances, and I have thought of a plan."

"I, too, have thought of one; perhaps it is the same as yours," said her husband.

"I, too, have considered a plan," said Adelbert; "and it is to marry the beautiful widow of Lothair; all trouble would then be at an end. I am willing to marry her, and believe I would have no trouble in winning her."

"That is exactly my plan," agreed Willa. "We will go immediately to work to bring it about. You may depend upon me to smooth the way; you can count upon your mother."

"There is one thing that troubles me," remarked the young man reflectively, "the curse of ugliness is upon my features. Lothair was exceptionally handsome. Adelheid will compare me with him, and these Burgundy people are self-willed and proud."

"She will never refuse such a chance as this," assured Willa. "You will be her choice above all others."

"Yes," agreed Berengarius, "we can win her without trouble; but if she should prove rebellious, it will be time enough to use harsh measures, but not in view of the people, only in stillness and secrecy."

"Perhaps at the right time she will call to memory what happened to her husband," remarked Willa with an evil smile, to which her husband agreed.

"Adelheid knows nothing of what happened in Pavia. I will go, my son, and ask her hand for you."

An hour later Berengarius visited the residence of Queen Adelheid, and asked for an audience. She appeared immediately in the reception-room, and he was admitted and made his errand known.

Adelheid gazed at him with a look of horror in her pale face, and for a time was unable to speak.

"My heart is bowed down with grief for the loss of a beloved husband," she said at length. "It is an insult to make such a proposition to me; it fills me with loathing, and is a shock to my tenderest feelings, for it is well known to me who was responsible for my husband's death."

"I am sorry that your Majesty has made the mistake of listening to idle and foolish reports," replied Berengarius with a look of injured innocence; "the gossip of people should have no weight with one of your high character. Now I ask you to remember that my son was made ruler over the kingdom of Italy; he offers you his hand, and it would be wise for you to accept."

Adelheid made no reply, but the look of abhorrence upon her face answered for her; and Berengarius left the palace in shame and anger.

10

✄ On Lake Garda ✄

AFTER THE DEPARTURE of Berengarius the young queen wept and sighed, completely abandoning herself to her grief; for not only was she filled with excitement over the unexpected visit, but tortured with anxiety, not knowing what revenge the father and son would visit upon her defenseless person.

She was buried in thought as to whom she could apply to for protection, when Hedwig, always her comforter, came in.

"Your Majesty," said she tenderly, "I was in my room, the door was ajar, and I heard the conversation between you and the caller, and could see him; he has an evil countenance."

"You heard the offer of marriage to his son?"

"Yes; and, *oh!* the look he cast at you when you refused; it was more like that of a beast of prey than that of a human being."

"I can expect nothing good of him nor of his godless wife," sobbed Adelheid, "but what can I do to turn them from such a frightful scheme? I am entirely in his power, and what can turn a king from anything he has determined upon?"

"We must take to flight," said Hedwig. "That is the only way of escape. A longer stay in Pavia would see you in prison."

"But where shall I go? Where can I find a place that is not upon the enemy's soil? I can take no steps that will not be watched by the spies of Berengarius."

"And for this reason there is the greatest need of haste. Before that tyrant and his wife can think of a plan to hinder your flight, we must turn our backs on Pavia."

"Listen, Hedwig! There is one place where we can go, and that is to my brother in Burgundy. With him I would be sure of protection; and, *oh!* my dear mother is there at this time." Tears of joy took the place of tears of terror.

"There is really no other place where you would be safe," replied Hedwig, trembling with hope and expectation. "It surely is a long distance from Pavia to our cherished fatherland, but we can walk it by resting on the way wherever we can find a hiding-place. Our first stopping-place would be Como. There no one would recognize us. By resting there, we will gain new strength to continue our journey. Compose yourself, your Majesty, while I gather some food and the few things we must have on our way."

That evening a spy was sent to the palace with an important message for the queen.

"She has gone out for a walk," said the attendant at the door.

"What direction did she take, and who accompanied her?"

"Only her favorite lady-in-waiting, and they went in the direction of Como."

The caller departed immediately upon receiving just the information he needed and expected.

With delight Berengarius ordered a number of fully armed men on swift horses to follow the fugitives, the king's displeasure to be visited upon them if they returned without her.

In the meantime the queen and Hedwig had reached a forest where they intended to remain through the day, while they would travel at night. In the midst of a thicket they slept the sleep of exhaustion.

Refreshed, they started again on their way and after much privation and weariness they reached Como to find the gates of the walled city closed against them; and horsemen waiting for them, who took them into custody.

"I have an order from the king to take you back to Pavia," said the leader. Adelheid made no resistance, but tears of despair rolled down her pale cheeks.

"This is a sad prospect for you, my Hedwig," she said, speaking German, which the soldiers could not understand. "I cannot expect you to share my trials. I will have no unkind feeling against you if you do not wish to stay with me."

"Your offer, my queen, does honor to you, hut I cannot accept it. Five happy years have I been with you, and you have shown me all kindness in your power, as has also your dear mother when she was at the palace. No, I can never forget your goodness to me; I could not live away from you."

"You true and faithful soul!" said the queen, kissing her. "Truly, how could I live without you?"

The leader noticed the friendship between the two, and, not understanding such an attachment between a queen and her maid, thought it best to make an explanation.

"I have no authority to take your maid back to Pavia," he said; "she must leave you."

"The king will surely not do such a wicked thing as to forbid her coming with me," exclaimed Adelheid, pale from fright; "for years she has been my dear companion."

"I do not know what the king will say to her coming. I have no command to bring her. Do not hinder us any longer, as he will be angry at the delay"; and he grasped the bridle of the queen's horse to set out for Pavia.

"Have pity on us!" cried Hedwig, weeping and holding out her hands to the horseman. "My beloved mistress needs me. Do not leave me here!" Grasping the bridle of his horse, she continued, "I will not let go until you say you will take me with you."

"Then I am compelled to use force to drive you away."

"Take your sword and kill me if you must; I would accept death as willingly as to be parted from my lady."

"You shall go with her. The king commanded me to bring Queen Adelheid, but did not command me to leave you. However, it makes some change in regard to the horses; you cannot walk and keep up with us."

This was done, and they turned in the direction of Pavia.

It was late at night when they reached Pavia, and as the leader had not been told where to leave his prisoners, he took them to the castle of Berengarius, and to the queen's grief and anxiety she found herself a prisoner in the power of a terrible tyrant and his covetous wife.

She was surprised to see their friendly manner toward her, and she had the hope that they had repented of the distress they had given her in proposing a marriage with their son.

"It was not kind of you to leave my protection," said Berengarius in what was meant to be a hospitable tone. "It would have been terrible if you had met robbers on the way. You should have a protector at all times, and there is no one who would be more suitable than my son Adelbert; I hope that you have decided to accept him."

"Be our dear daughter, Adelheid, and every earthly happiness will be yours," said Willa with her treacherous smile.

But the young queen scorned the offer, and the faces of husband and wife paled with anger.

"If kindness has no effect, then we must use harsh measures"; and Berengarius struck her with such force that it was only with great effort that she kept from falling.

"Will you do as we wish?" he exclaimed in a loud, rough voice, raising his hand as though about to strike her another blow.

"No, I would rather die."

"Do you realize that you are entirely in our power?"

"Yes, and you can poison me as you did my husband; then I will be out of your way."

"That is good advice," he said, and beside himself with rage, he threw her roughly into an adjoining apartment, where she was really a prisoner, for the windows were barricaded, and he locked the door.

But there was one blessing left her for which she gave grateful thanks to God — Hedwig shared her prison, and together they wept and prayed.

⌒ ❋ ⌒

At midnight and in the darkness of a cloudy night a troop of horsemen passed through the gate of the walled city of Pavia. They were soldiers, well armed, wearing helmets and chain armors. In the center of the group rode two female figures, closely veiled and mantled, a soldier holding the bridle of each horse.

As soon as the company passed into the open, they put the horses to a quick gait, and at the same time cast glances about them as if expecting attack from some quarter.

They had traveled a long distance, when one of the soldiers spoke to the one nearest him.

"I see no need of so much secrecy," he said in a low tone, "on such a dark night as this there is not the least danger of meeting hindrances."

"No; I see no use in being so cautious; but we must obey orders. Perhaps there is a reason for secrecy greater than we know."

"If we only knew who these women are, and why they are so closely veiled, we might have some idea of the reason; but we cannot catch the least glimpse of their faces. They have not spoken, except a few words, and in a language we cannot understand."

"Listen, comrade," said the other, "I believe these women are Queen Adelheid and her maid, have you thought of this?"

"No; and if you wish to pass the rest of your life in a dark dungeon or have a dose of poison in you, I advise you to keep your thoughts to yourself. With this new king we must guard our tongues."

"If it were not the persons I speak of, why need our leader be so secret about it? And who but some distinguished person would have such a number of soldiers to guard them?"

His opinion was correct; the prisoners were Queen Adelheid and Hedwig. A little before midnight they were awakened from their restless sleep, and taken out in the darkness of the night, they knew not where, the secrecy of it filling their hearts with terror.

"Dark as this terrible night are my fears for the future," said the queen in the German tongue as they rode along; "Berengarius and his wife Willa see in my marriage with their son a strengthening of their not entirely secure claim to the throne. They know well that I have friends and adherents that would stand by me were I to assert my rights to it, and there is no doubt in my mind that I, too, will disappear from the world's stage as did my poor husband. It must be something of this kind that I am taken out at midnight and guarded by so many horsemen. It is all the work of that infamous tiger and his infamous wife."

"Take comfort in the thought, my queen, that your friends and adherents will not let this matter rest, but will come to your assistance."

"I cannot hope for it. Who will know where I am taken, or know that I am among the living? Berengarius and his wife will take care that no one will know where I am imprisoned.

"Berengarius is now owner of my castles and strongholds, and over all of them he has absolute authority."

"If we cannot count upon man's help, let us turn to God Almighty," said Hedwig. "He has a thousand ways to help us of which man knows nothing, and can in His own good time deliver you from all your troubles."

"You are right, Hedwig. That is real trouble that prompts us to trust implicitly in God the All-wise and the almighty Helper. I will rely upon Him to do what is best for me."

At daylight the cavalcade halted for rest and food in a forest, and then resumed the journey.

On the evening of the third day they reached a wild, mountainous region. Great rocks reared their heads in the air, already damp from the mists of the evening. They rode for more than a mile through a rocky path, and upon a high point of rocky land they saw the outlines of an ancient castle.

"Now I know exactly where we are," said a soldier to the one next to him. "It is Garda Castle, on Garda Lake, which is seven miles long."

"Do not betray your trust," whispered his companion. "Eager ears are listening, and it may bear evil fruit to you. You know as well as I that we are threatened with heavy punishment if we speak of any events of this long and tedious journey."

"It is Garda Castle," whispered the queen to Hedwig. "I have heard and read of it; it is the most solitary and remote fortress in the kingdom. We will indeed have a dreary place to live here, perhaps for life."

The keeper of the gate evidently knew of their coming. The gate was open, and the cavalcade passed into the courtyard, then through a dark passageway to the entrance to the castle, where the steward received them.

The steward was a blinded servitor of the new king, and Adelheid knew that whatever commands he had received in regard to them would be followed. He received her with scant courtesy, and conducted her and Hedwig to her apartment.

"You are from this evening on a prisoner of Castle Garda," he said austerely, "and I have orders to hold you with rigid firmness. I have others to assist me if you rebel. It is an undeserved favor that the king allows you to have your maid with you. Now follow me."

They passed down a long, narrow corridor, then down a long flight of steps into a small, musty room, the rough stone walls of which were moist, and with a stone floor. A small window near the vaulted ceiling spread a dim light. There was a rough wooden couch, two rough chairs, a table, and an earthen water-jug.

"You can be very comfortable here," the steward said, "much more so than you deserve for your refusal to marry the king's son. Food and drink will be brought to you, but you need not expect dainties, for you will not have them."

As the rough and heartless man left the place, the queen sank down upon the couch and wept bitterly, and Hedwig joined in her grief, which seemed hopeless of relief.

"It adds to my sorrow to have you suffer here with me," said Adelheid. "For all I know to the contrary, I may be imprisoned for life. I know that I should not expect you to stay with me, yet my heart chills at the thought of being alone."

"Can you imagine, my queen, that I could leave you? No; in life and death I am with you. What could I do if I left you? I have no home nor any employment, so in remaining with you I am receiving as much favor as I am giving. Moreover, I am sure they would not let me go, knowing that I would betray your place of imprisonment if set free."

"Oh, Hedwig, I thank God for the comfort you have always been to me," replied the queen gratefully. "This place will not seem like a prison if you are with me."

Long they conversed that evening of the happy days when King Lothair lived and they were so happy together, and the time did not pass so heavily. But there were days when Adelheid wept and prayed for deliverance from the dark and dreary place, and Hedwig would weep with her.

One day the rusty key grated in the lock, the door opened, and the chaplain of the castle entered the dimly lighted apartment. He was young, strong in frame, and tall in stature, and, *oh!* to the joy of the queen and Hedwig was able to speak German as well as Italian.

His cheerful voice and manner were like a sunbeam in the somber room, and gave a ray of hope to the lonely, helpless women, who had seen no one from the outside world since their imprisonment.

"My name is Martin," he said, "and I am chaplain in Garda Castle. It is my duty and pleasure to visit any prisoners in the castle, and give them the comfort of our blessed Christian religion. It was some time before I could persuade the steward to allow me to visit you, but at last he gave permission, and so I was free to come."

His visit was a benediction to them; an angel's visit could have been scarcely more welcome. His hearty cheerfulness gave them courage, and they felt that they had at least one friend in the world.

After giving them the blessed comfort of Christ's own words, he engaged in conversation about worldly affairs; of his experiences in life outside and in Garda Castle, and time passed swiftly as he talked. Bidding them goodbye, he promised to call again, leaving them more cheered and hopeful than they had thought possible.

11

⚸ Garda Castle ⚸

THE IMPRISONMENT of Queen Adelheid, which Berengarius and his wife supposed to be a secret known only to themselves, was soon spread abroad in Italy, and after a little time reached Germany.

Early in the summer of 951 Duke Henry of Bavaria came to visit his brother. King Otto, who was at that time at his castle at Merseburg, and to tell him of what had happened at Pavia, in Italy.

They had heard of the death of King Lothair and the imprisonment of the helpless young queen, and they had known for years of the rapacious Berengarius and his vicious wife, who had been working to secure the crown of Italy, and would not stop at crime to gain their end.

Long and earnestly the brothers conversed about the doings in Italy.

"Lothair was in the way of Berengarius," remarked Duke Henry, "and he is strongly suspected of ending the poor young king's life. Queen Adelheid is in his way, and he knows that, as long as she lives, the crown upon his head is far from secure; and her imprisonment bodes evil for her."

"He intends, without doubt, to keep her a prisoner for life," rejoined King Otto. "Our father was always on the best of terms with Burgundy, and it is my duty to protect the hapless queen and not leave her to her fate. I will without delay call together the representative men of my kingdom, and lay the case before them."

"I would, and you will find that to a man they will be with you heart and soul."

"Our father, King Henry, as you know, always had a longing to bring Italy, the Roman Empire, back to all the splendor which reigned there in the days of our great fore-father, Charles the Great, Charlemagne; perhaps the opportunity has come to fulfill this desire."

"It is just the time," rejoined Duke Henry. "Now, Otto, act quickly, and reach that long-wished-for aim. Make Adel-heid your wife; it has been four years since your loved Editha passed away, and you are but forty years of age. To the dif-ference in your age and hers, I am sure, she will not object. She will not only give you her hand, but her heart. You will win not only a beautiful and loving wife, but the kingdom of Italy; and she will win not only a faithful husband, but a powerful protector."

"Berengarius has no thought of help from this quarter; I will be glad to show him his mistake," remarked the king reflectively.

"Of course, he will struggle to retain the crown, but his opposition to you will be of no avail. I will exert my every power to aid you to extinguish him."

"You have suggested something that has reason for a foundation, and I thank you for it. Now Kabald, what do you think of Duke Henry's proposition?" he said, turning to his chamberlain.

"I agree entirely with his Highness Duke Henry. You have had suggestions for marriage from different quarters, but your kingdom and its interests were uppermost in your mind; its power and greatness were your supreme consider-ation."

"Adelheid's beauty and piety are everywhere spoken of," remarked Duke Henry. "Happy will it be for you to win her love and, with her, the inheritance of the throne of King Lothair of Italy."

"You have for years been a good friend and wise coun-selor to me, Henry, and have caused me to forget all that you once intended against me. In the stillness of my church I will ask God's blessing upon what will come to pass, if it be His will. Now, through the representative men of the kingdom we will call an army together for the release of the young queen from prison; and the duty devolves upon you, Kabald, to call upon them to raise an army."

"This I will do joyfully," said the chamberlain. "I will send messengers through the length and breadth of the German kingdom, to the governors of the cities, to the military leaders, and to all others that should be notified, informing them of a gathering-place."

This was done, and enthusiasm filled every German heart. They realized the glory that would come to their realm should they release the lonely young queen of Italy from the power of a tyrannical oppressor.

Swords, clubs, battle-axes, lances, spears, arrows, helmets, and chained armors of mail were jubilantly prepared for the march across the Alps into Italy.

No one was more interested in the affair than was Ludolph, the son of Otto, who in 948 had been made Duke of Swabia. He hurried to Merseburg to see his father, and hear of the gathering of an army to battle for the liberation of Queen Adelheid. He was also anxious to see his dear friend Hildeward, and tell him of a plan by which the queen could be liberated before the army could be collected and wished his friend to join with him.

This twenty-year-old duke was never forgetful that his life had been saved by that faithful friend Hildeward, and he loved him for his real and true friendship, his agreeable and cheering society, and his clear reasoning in matters which he could not decide for himself. When their views differed, he felt no resentment, no wounded pride or irritation that Hildeward advised against his plans.

In this new plan he certainly did admonish, with all the strength he could put into his words, against such a senseless scheme.

"My dear friend," said Prince Ludolph, the moment they were alone, "I have a splendid plan in view for which I want your help; I want you to join me in collecting an army and march across the Alps to the Garda Castle and free Queen Adelheid from prison."

"How could your Highness do this?" asked Hildeward quietly, not wishing to dampen the young man's enthusiasm until he had heard the whole story.

"You do not seem to enter joyously into it, as I expected," continued Ludolph, "but I have this confidence in you that you will not be against me if you cannot help me, and will not divulge what I am about to tell you, and so I will speak to you openly and candidly.

"After consulting with distinguished friends of mine, I have decided to go with a small company of Swabian soldiers to Italy and free the queen before my father can collect his army. I know that my zeal and well-accomplished plan will surprise and delight my father, and save him much expense and trouble, he will be proud to call me his son, and more than that, the world will praise my valor. My father cannot collect an army and march to Garda Castle before the last of September, and long before that the work will all be done, and the queen will be free. Now I expect you to join with me, and share my work and the honor that will be ours."

"Forgive me, my dear and honored Prince Ludolph. I really could not join in this undertaking, and I wish you would not think of it. It would not surprise and please your father, but would shame and anger him. Do not let your youthful zeal lead you into such a foolish attempt, which would end in regret to yourself."

"But how could it end that way? I will take good care to make it a success. Come with me, Hildeward. You will be sorry when you find people applauding my great deed."

"Berengarius will get word of your intention, my gracious duke, and will collect a much larger army than yours. He is on the spot, while you are far away, and will be weary from the hardships entailed in crossing the Alps. It would be a failure, and do great injury to the queen's cause."

"I see that you are opposed to it," said Prince Ludolph, greatly disappointed, "but I will not change my plans. I know that your advice is well meant, but this time your objections are useless. The scheme has taken deep root in my mind, and a great number of friends and adherents are eager to have me undertake it. I would be very much pleased to see you go with me, and I hope that of your own free will you will change your mind. But in any case, my father must know nothing of it, at least not until we are on our way to Italy."

"Did you let your uncle, Duke Henry of Bavaria, into the secret?"

"No; nor must he be given a hint of it. We have, as you may have noticed, not the love for each other that one should expect of near relatives. He always makes objections to my plans, and I get angry. He wishes to play the part of guardian over me, and looks upon me as an irresponsible boy. He forgets that I am Duke of Swabia and the only heir to the German crown."

Hildeward's spirits brightened at hearing this, for he believed that the foolish plan would come to the knowledge of Duke Henry, and that thus the disaster would be averted. But there was no time for further discussion, for a servant came to tell him that the king wished him to come to his apartment.

"I have an important commission for you, Hildeward," he said, "a commission that will prove my confidence in you. As it is not possible to send my army to Italy before the last of September, I feel that Queen Adelheid should know that she is to be released from her prison. It will give her hope and be a bright spot in her dreary life there; and I have chosen you to take the message to her. Your sagacity and prudence will be called into play on this errand, and I feel confident that you will be successful. A failure would cause her to be secretly removed to another place. She is now at Garda Castle, which overlooks Garda Lake, and the place is strictly guarded; therefore it will be no easy task to get my message into her own hands. Now I ask you if you are willing to undertake this difficult, perhaps dangerous mission."

With real delight Hildeward accepted the charge, such an adventure being a joy to his energetic nature. But above all was he pleased to see that King Otto put so much confidence in him; it was an acknowledgment of his ability. He therefore gratefully thanked him for selecting him for such an important mission.

"You must have someone as protector on the long journey," said the king, "and I will leave it to you to choose whomsoever you wish."

"I am sure I will not need protection, my gracious king, but I would be glad to have the company of my uncle Gozbert. His experience and his fearlessness are a tonic to anyone."

"An excellent selection," commented the king heartily, "the old hunter will be a help in every way."

Uncle Gozbert's heart thrilled with delight at the prospect of a journey to Italy. "Yes," he said, "with my heart's love, Hildeward, I would travel through thick and thin to the end of the world."

There were no great preparations to be made for the journey, and on the second day they set out, well armed, upon strong horses, and bearing a letter from King Otto to Queen Adelheid. A pack of food and clothing was loaded on each horse.

The journey was not an easy one, for there were no roads. Their way led through briars, and rocks, morass and mire, and dense forests, and the horses carried them over deep streams and brooks, bridges being scarce. When night came, they frequently had no place to sleep except beside the trunk of a fallen tree, or sometimes on deep grass. At times they would find a cave large enough to accommodate both, which was a welcome retreat. The horses would be tethered close by. Very rarely they reached a huntsman's cabin, where they were cordially welcomed, or a deserted cloister, where they had a long night's sleep and rest.

Frequently, in forests, they were compelled to pass the night in a tree to escape the wolves, bears, or other wild animals. Nevertheless, they cheerfully continued their journey, their aim always in mind.

In spite of all difficulties they, in the early part of July, found themselves on Italian soil, and it was not a difficult task to find Garda Castle. At evening, on a rainy day, they found themselves in sight of it, and in a fisherman's cabin, on the shore of the lake, they found shelter for the night.

They would have been glad to listen to some information in regard to the castle, but the fisherman could not understand a word of German nor they of Italian; so there was nothing to be learned of him.

They soon realized that to deliver the king's letter into Queen Adelheid's hand was the most difficult part of the undertaking, and when several days had passed, they saw themselves no nearer the aim than on the first day.

"We must try another plan if we are to accomplish anything," said Gozbert after three days of watching, searching, lying in wait, and exploring. "I have thought of a plan to get myself into the castle. Tomorrow I will stir up a quarrel with the four men who go with a mule-cart to buy food and other things for the castle. It would be a light job to fight them all, but I will let them arrest me, and take me a prisoner to the castle-prison. I will at least be inside the place and may see something that may be in our favor. If they seem on the point of killing me, then you can come, and I will let them see what a German sword or German fists can do."

"But the letter, uncle! Would it not be dangerous to take it into the castle with you in case you are searched?"

"Yes, it will be better to leave it with you. You may have a chance to get the letter into the queen's hand; if not, we will feel that we have done all in our power, and the queen will have to remain in prison until the king's troops come to release her."

"But, uncle, it will be of no advantage to you to be a prisoner, and, perhaps, to be thrust into a dark dungeon; that would be terrible for a man of your age. Let me be the one to be arrested."

"No! I would suffer the anguish of death to know that you were a prisoner in a dungeon; but we will let destiny or chance decide for us by leaving it to blades of grass."

He took a long and a short one, and putting one in each, hand behind his back, he said, "Right or left for the long blade?"

"Right," said Hildeward, and it was his place to attack the mule-drivers.

"I will be near you," said Gozbert, "and if I see that there is danger of your being overpowered, I will come on them like a hail-storm. If they arrest you and take you into the castle, I will keep still, and pray the Lord to protect you."

As soon as the plan was decided upon, and while waiting for a cart to pass by, Hildeward told his uncle of the exploit which young Prince Ludolph had in view.

"Watch for him, uncle, as he may be here at any time. I strongly advised against it, but my warning had no effect upon him. He will be in great danger. Pray for his safety, and protect him as well as you can."

"I promise you, for that boy is the pride of many hearts. He is a hot-headed, blustering youth, but noble at heart and beloved of all Germany. Rest assured that I will protect him at the risk of my own life. The foolish, foolish boy to imagine that he can free the queen from such a man as Berengarius!"

Shortly before the time the cart was to pass by on its daily errand, the two secreted themselves behind a rock and upon its return, when the cart was loaded with provisions and fruit, Hildeward sprang out and made a feint of robbery. He was immediately attacked by the four men, whom he fought off, then, apparently overpowered, was made a prisoner and taken into the castle as a spy.

"Search him," said the steward. "Let not a fold of his clothes escape your notice."

This was done, but nothing was found as the king's letter was in Gozbert's possession.

"There was no reason to think him a spy," said the steward; "but he deserves to be a prisoner for trying to rob the cart. A spy would not be likely to attack mule-drivers. Say, youngster, what have you to say for yourself?"

Hildeward made an answer, but it was not understood by any of the Italians waiting to hear.

"To all appearances the boy is a German. Does he not know the danger of coming to this land at this time? I wish I could understand his language; I would like to have a talk with him. The chaplain talks to the queen in some foreign language, which may be German. Through the queen's maid I can find out if this boy is a German."

Hedwig was summoned, and the delight of brother and sister after their long separation was past expression; and quickly he gave her from memory the full and correct message of the king. Then for a moment he could chat of their own affairs.

The steward saw that they were really brother and sister, and was satisfied. How the brother had learned that his sister was a prisoner at Castle Garda he had not taken into consideration.

The moment the steward told Hedwig to return to her cell, she fled with the joyful news that King Otto would bring an army to free the queen; and their dungeon grew bright with this gladdening assurance.

Hildeward realized that he, too, would be a prisoner until released by King Otto; but his only regret was that he could not see his uncle Gozbert, and tell him that the queen had received the message.

12

⚜ The Haunted Tower ⚜

N THE WEEKS that had passed since Queen Adelheid and Hedwig were prisoners in Garda Castle, the chaplain visited their dungeon as often as he could without neglecting any of his many duties. He had deep sympathy for them in their helpless condition, and did all in his power to cheer them with the assurance that God was watching over them, and in His own good time would liberate them.

He not only encouraged them, but watched for an opportunity to help them to gain their freedom.

"Dear friend," said Adelheid one day, "do you really think it not possible for us to be freed from this terrible imprisonment? You are so kind to us that I am sure you would be glad to see us free, and are so considerate and resourceful that you surely can see some way to help us to escape."

"I would gladly help, did I see any possible way; but this castle is so secure as to walls, doors, and windows that it is simply impossible to escape through them; and since your Majesty's coming the number of sentinels has been increased to such an extent that a cat could not pass in or out without being noticed. The steward is a faithful servitor of King Berengarius, and is watchful at every point. But do not be discouraged; something may occur to our advantage, and I will be on the lookout for it."

"Are not soldiers held as prisoners here who might be willing to help you to get us out?" asked Hedwig.

"Child, consider what you are saying! Whom would I

dare entrust with such an undertaking? Should they betray us, the king would soon hear of it, and our heads would not be long upon our shoulders. Just think of the many sentinels that surround this castle!"

"Could not a wall in an obscure part of the castle be broken through, large enough for us to pass out?" asked the queen tearfully.

"It might be done, your Majesty, with the help of some-one of the men whom one dare trust. But what could be done with the heap of stones and mortar which would not fail to be seen by sentinels outside and guards inside the castle?" Hedwig said nothing in reply, but the thought that came to her was, "If I were a man, I would find a way."

Several days passed, and the subject was not mentioned again until a few days before the coming of Hildeward with the joyful news that they were to be liberated by King Otto, when one day the chaplain came at an unaccustomed hour to the queen's dungeon, looking pale and anxious.

"I have some sad news for you, gracious queen," he said. "I would gladly spare you the anxiety, but it cannot be kept a secret."

"You frighten me, Martin," and her pale, lovely face grew paler; "but tell me whatever it may be; I can bear it. Any change would be better than this terrible dungeon."

"An hour ago I was in a small room that adjoins the apartment of the steward. A messenger sent by King Berengarius was announced. The door being slightly ajar, I heard the conversation, and it made my blood run cold. The king's orders were that you be kept a prisoner for life, and that the steward and his wife are to supply you with only the most necessary things, as in prison you would require very little. The king added that he placed full confidence in the steward to obey his orders implicitly. Then, in return, the king was sent a message by the steward to the effect that he would do exactly as commanded, and asked if he wished the queen's maid and her spiritual adviser retained; for if so, he believed that the queen's imprisonment would be greatly shortened. The messenger promised to lay the matter before the king and report as soon as possible."

The queen wrung her hands in despair, and Hedwig wept in anguish of mind.

"A reply cannot reach the steward before three weeks," continued Martin, "and in that time a way may be opened for escape."

The queen, however, was hopeless.

"Do not despair, gracious lady. We have no reason to give up hope; on the contrary, we must seriously think of ways and means of escape. I am ready to risk my life to save you from enduring this shameful treatment, and I believe that God will show us a way."

The morning before Hildeward was arrested and brought into the castle, the chaplain came with a happy expression upon his face to tell the queen and Hedwig that he had found a means of escape. He did not deny that the plan was fraught with danger, but by the help of the Almighty, and if they were cautious and persevering, it might be done.

"Speak, speak! Tell us all about it!" said the queen, her face flushing with delight, while Hedwig's eyes were filled with tears of joy.

"As you know, in the capacity of chaplain I am at liberty to go over the castle and have keys to the prisoners' rooms. I searched the walls for a place where the stones might be removed, but found none. In the courtyard, however, in a remote corner, there is an ancient tower, almost in a state of collapse. It was built in pagan times, and it has long ago outlived its usefulness. Going through it, I found that in one of the basement-rooms, used in early times as a cellar, there is a place where the wall might be broken through, which would let one out on the bank of the lake. The old tower is not guarded, neither from the castle nor from outside. The best of it is that its walls are of sandstone, and it will not be much trouble to break through them."

"Oh, the joy of seeing a hope of escape from the power of the man who murdered my husband, and would do the same by me," said Adelheid, clasping her hands in thanksgiving.

"I really see reason for great hope," said the chaplain cheerfully, "and I will mention another point in our favor.

In this tower there is at intervals a subterranean sound, like a groan or a long-drawn sigh, and sometimes a rushing sound as of huge wings. Of course, the servants and even the steward believe it to be haunted, and will not go near it night or day, which is greatly in our favor. Of course, the sounds are easily accounted for. No doubt, there is running water under the flooring, which causes the rushing, roaring, and groaning; the moaning and whistling may be accounted for in the same way.

"This superstitious belief kept the old tower from being demolished, which is of great advantage just now, for it will keep all interlopers at a safe distance while the wall is being broken."

"Oh, Martin, dear friend, can you really do this to help us out of prison" Have you the strength needed for such a task?"

"God will give me strength"; and his fine eyes beamed with enthusiasm and energy, while the queen and Hedwig felt almost happy at the prospect of being free.

The next day was the day of Hildeward's arrest and the happy meeting of brother and sister, as well as the giving of the message for the queen. Their dear friend, the chaplain, was told all when he made his next visit.

"There is no need now of your exerting yourself to break an opening into the wall," said the queen cheerfully. "The powerful ruler of the German kingdom will meet Berengarius with a great army; he will he overpowered, and we will be free. We can well endure the few weeks we must stay here when we need not look forward to life-imprisonment."

"Your Majesty must not be deterred by this good news from making the effort to escape;' he said. "No doubt, the noble German king will carry out his great-hearted plan, but the danger to you is in no way set aside; rather it is greatly increased."

"How can that be?" inquired Adelheid, her sweet face taking on the look of care and anxiety which for a little while had left it.

"It cannot be long concealed from Berengarius what the German king is intending to do, and you would be taken from here secretly, and not to any public place or well-known castle, but to some hidden spot, where it would be impossible to trace you."

"The chaplain is right," said Hedwig with pale lips; "we must not stay here."

"It is only in quick flight that your Majesty can expect safety," rejoined the chaplain. "The walls of this castle must be at our backs before Berengarius has time to send you to another place. In four or six days, I hope, we will be on the way to freedom; for I, too, must flee, as I am already suspected by the steward, as evinced by his message to the king, and I would suffer from the ax of the executioner. I feel certain that God will bless our efforts to escape."

"He has already blessed us," said Hedwig, "by sending my brother Hildeward; he is young and strong and will gladly help."

"He, too, will get his freedom by helping you," said the chaplain. "I will visit him in my capacity as spiritual adviser, and tell him of my plans."

It seemed to Hedwig the escape was assured because Hildeward could assist the chaplain, and her good spirits cheered the queen.

"I was especially fortunate this morning, while searching the old tower, to find a stone slab not too large and heavy for me to remove with a lever," continued the chaplain. "I raised it and found it covered an orifice which in early times had been a fountain and was a subterranean opening into the lake, and the water flowing in and out caused the moaning and rumbling which alarms the inmates of the castle. The finding of it is of great advantage, for in its great depth can be thrown all the rubbish from the broken wall."

The next day, when the chaplain made his daily visits to the prisoners, he gave Hildeward a full account of his plan. The young man listened with strict attention. He saw the extreme need of the queen's being liberated, and with her his sister, the chaplain, and himself. He was impatient for night to come on, that they might commence their work on the wall.

During the day the chaplain secured a pike, a crow-bar,

an ax, and a pine torch, and a covering for the doorway to keep the dim light from being seen outside.

Hedwig was to keep watch inside the door-covering, to give warning if there were danger ahead, and a signal for the work to cease.

"I really think there is no danger of being discovered," said the chaplain, "for, the wind being high to-night, there will be less likelihood of the pounding and boring being noticed; yet it will give us a feeling of security to know that a good friend is keeping guard over us."

Cautiously and silently the three left their rooms, crept from the castle, and crossed the courtyard to the old tower. They felt it to be another divine blessing that the night was dark, moonless, and cloudy.

The chaplain had provided a rope, with a stone securely tied at one end of it, which they were to take to the cellar room, and the other end of the rope was held in Hedwig's hand. If there seemed to be any danger, she would draw the rope as a signal to cease working. Hildeward handled the tools with a skill and energy that surprised the chaplain, who was kept busy carrying away the rubbish and dropping it down the opening, the noise not being heard because of the roaring of the wind.

On those short August nights they could work but an hour with safety, which would make it necessary to work at least five nights, judging by what they had accomplished in one. But they were not discouraged.

They had been employed but half an hour when Hedwig heard the sound of a man's footsteps, and she drew the rope while all three listened.

"Now what do you suppose is making that noise in the tower?" asked one of the sentinels of another. "I have never heard that sound before."

"The evil spirits in the walls are weary of the groaning and moaning and are trying pounding. This is the first time we' have heard them, and it is not so frightful as the groans."

"It makes my hair stand up on my head with terror when I hear them, for we do not know what harm they can do."

Long before dawn Martin and Hildeward ceased their work, and the three glided through the corridors to their cells without being discovered.

Martin dropped into slumber immediately, but was awakened at an early hour by a messenger of the castle bringing him a request from the steward, which he received with anxiety, believing that the work in the tower had been discovered. His limbs trembled, for he knew the stern keeper's regard for duty, and also knew the penalty of treason to the king.

"I sent for you," said the steward the moment he appeared, "to tell you that the sentinels report that there were sounds in the old tower that have never before been heard."

"What kind of sounds?" asked the chaplain, his heart thumping so fiercely that he feared the steward would notice it.

"It is a pounding, grating, and hammering; and it is my duty to see that the cause be removed. The evil spirits must be exorcized, as it is my duty to see that nothing to shock the senses has possession of the ghost tower."

"Have you been there to see for yourself where the sound was located?"

"Not I; you must go with me, chaplain; a godless spirit will not come near a spiritual man like you, while it would have no respect for me, nor for anyone in the castle. Come with me, with your spiritual coat of mail, which they will not touch. You will be a protection to me."

Martin could not see for a moment any way out of this difficulty, and a cold moisture was on his forehead; but the Lord had come to his aid in many emergencies, and he believed it would not fail him now. Apparently willing, he agreed to go.

"But," said he, after taking a few steps, "should we not, upon reflection, be satisfied that the tormented spirits remain in their own haunts, and never invade the castle to frighten us" Will it not be better to keep peace with them by being willing to allow them to change their manner of complaining? The pounding and hammering are no more disagreeable to listen to than the sighs and groans and roaring; and we should make no effort to disturb them, but let them alone in their old tower."

This accorded exactly with the opinion of the steward. He did not have to risk an invasion of those quarters of the tormented spirits. The chaplain, too, was satisfied that there would be no need of Hedwig's watching; for the new way the evil spirits were showing their power increased the terror of the ghost tower with every attendant at the castle.

On the fourth evening of their work upon the wall, though it was very thick, the opening was large enough for Hildeward to put his feet through, and they felt that they had made fair progress. It was easier work than at first, although their hands were blistered from the unaccustomed toil.

But this was of small consideration, the chaplain's only worry being how to keep his hands out of sight of the steward, so that no awkward questions difficult to answer might be asked. It had been no small task to take the refuse to the vault, but he did it gladly, as the release of the young Italian queen was his earnest concern, and an aching back, which deprived him of sleep, was of small consideration.

In the fifth night they succeeded in making the orifice large enough to allow the queen's and Hedwig's slender bodies to slip through. But for the chaplain's well-proportioned form and Hildeward's broad shoulders much more stone and mortar would have to be removed. On the morning of the sixth day the chaplain gave the queen and Hedwig the welcome news that they could that night pass through the outlet into freedom.

"Have everything ready for your flight," he said to Hedwig. "I will call for you. Hildeward is on the watch outside the wall, and by God's blessing we will turn our backs on Garda Castle and by daylight be out of sight of it."

"We can go to Reggio," whispered the queen, her beautiful face radiant with joy. "There lives the noble Bishop Adelard, who will help us to reach whatever place he and you decide upon as being a safe retreat."

The night of the twentieth of August was especially favorable for the escape. A high wind was raging around the great castle, and the weather-vanes on the towers rattled and screeched like the evil spirits supposed to be in the ghost tower. An hour after midnight, Martin quietly unlocked the doors of the two cells, and the three glided silently through the corridors and out of a seldom used small door into the courtyard and the ghost tower.

Martin bore on his shoulders a sack, in which were the provisions he could secure, and other necessary articles, among them a cowl, a doublet, and a suit of soldier's clothes. A stiletto was in his belt, and a sword at his side, of which he could make expert use. Hildeward also had a sack upon his shoulders in which were the belongings of Queen Adelheid and Hedwig, and of his own possessions there was the iron spike used in breaking through the wall, which could be used as a weapon if needed.

They went through the orifice without difficulty, and, *oh!* the joy it gave to the queen and Hedwig to breathe the air of freedom. As they passed down the rocky and steep path that led to the lake, Hildeward lent his strength to the safety of the queen, while the chaplain took care of Hedwig.

The fugitives did not halt in their walk until at daylight they reached a dense forest, where Hildeward found hiding-places for the queen and her maid, and, not far from them, places for themselves, where, totally exhausted, they slept the whole day.

In the meantime, it was also daylight at the castle and the servants were astir, but as the queen took breakfast when the day was quite advanced, the escape was not known until the sun had for several hours enlivened the earth with its beams.

It was the old deaf male servant who always took the morning meal to Queen Adelheid and Hedwig that found the dungeon empty, and as quickly as he could he made the escape known.

"It is impossible!" exclaimed the steward, pale with fright. "You must be beside yourself!" He ran to the queen's apartment, found it deserted, and the two cots untouched.

It could not happen unless one or more of the sentinels had been traitors to the king. No; it must be an evil stroke of magic, as they would not risk their lives when they could gain nothing thereby.

He gave the customary signal, and the sentinel on the tower gave forth mighty tones from the horn to summon the soldiers of that fortified stronghold to gather in the court-yard.

From all directions they hastened to the steward; for such a signal meant that there must be no delay. One of the soldiers hurried to the room of Hildeward, and as quickly returned.

"The German prisoner is gone," he said in real distress of mind.

"You scoundrel!" thundered the steward. "Where were you when he escaped?"

"I locked his room, as I always do, and it was locked when I went to give him his breakfast," replied the fright-ened guard.

The same report came from the guard of the queen's cell; the door was locked, but she and Hedwig were not to be found.

Every corner of the castle was searched to find the queen, but without success.

"Run to the chaplain's room, and tell him to come and give me advice as to what is best to be done."

The guard went, but came back with the report that the chaplain was not within, and the bed untouched.

This was an astonishing discovery. The chaplain was not a prisoner, why should he run away? The steward sent men in all directions to search for him, but all returned without bringing any knowledge of him.

"Have you looked in the ghost tower?" the steward asked.

"No; he would not go there. He is just as much afraid of it as we are. There was no use to look in there."

"Cowards, poltroons! Come with me, or it will cost your heads. The ghost tower must be searched!"

Saying this, he went with them to the tower, but all of them crossed themselves, and asked the protection of the Virgin.

The moment they entered, the moaning and roaring was heard, and they would have fled, had they not feared the steward's anger. He, too, halted, but kept on his way, and descended to the lower room. There he saw the big hole in the wall.

"There is where they escaped," he said. "The chaplain and that German coxcomb made that hole, and the queen and her maid escaped. That pious sneak and hypocrite Martin helped them do the work. I could dash my head against the wall for not suspecting him when he explained to me that the change in the sounds heard in the tower was as pleasant as the groaning, and that it would be better to have them remain there than to invade the castle. That was a ruse to keep us all away, so that they might accomplish their work."

"Do not worry about it, steward," said one of the guards. "Had the evil spirits not been in the tower, the prisoners would still be in their cells. It was the evil spirits that helped them," and he crossed himself, "or how could Chaplain Martin and that boy carry away all the stone and mortar that come from that great hole in the wall? You see no sign of it."

"You are right, and this is a comfort to me; against the power of evil spirits we poor souls have no power. But we are wasting time," and he ran up to the courtyard to consult with the men whom the tower sentinel had summoned with the horn.

"Mount your horses immediately, and hurry off to find the prisoners! They cannot be far away. It would be nearly morning before they could start, and the queen is not used to walking. Divide in four companies, and go in different directions. The one lucky enough to find the queen will receive a liberal reward. Hurry, men! In less than fifteen minutes you must be scouring the country in search of the fugitives."

The men rushed to the stalls for their horses, and in less time than had been given them they were galloping down the steep, narrow path that led from the castle, and as soon as they had reached the level ground, they sped away in every direction.

When they returned in the evening, they were compelled to report that they had seen nothing of the four, and could suggest no way to search further. The steward realized that he must report to the king, now at Verona, of the escape, and must go himself instead of sending a messenger.

As was to be supposed, Berengarius was beside himself with rage.

"She may have gone to Reggio," he said when he had grown a little calmer. "Bishop Adelard lives there, and they are great friends. I will send my soldiers there, and have them search the fields and forests; they cannot have gone far."

This was done, but without success, although at times the searchers were very near them. From their hiding-place the fugitives would sometimes see a solitary horseman spying carefully about him, but they were not discovered. Their place of refuge, where they secured a day's rest, often was a field where the grain grew to the height of a man.

Sometimes in the early hours of the morning they could hear the voices of the persons searching for them coming nearer and nearer, and they kept perfectly still.

"It seems to me," said one of the soldiers, "that the evil spirits of Garda are protecting these people, otherwise they could not hide so that we cannot find them."

"This is what all of us believe. We will never find them; the spirits will not allow it."

The fugitives were motionless, scarcely allowing themselves to breathe. The chaplain and Hildeward placed their hands upon their swords until the horsemen were out of sight.

Once, while hidden under a clump of dried leaves in the forest, the hoof of one of the horses was within a foot of Queen Adelheid.

It seemed that the eyes of the enemy were holden; for they passed on. The four arose and unitedly thanked God for His mercy and loving-kindness; and the queen repeated the words: *Call upon Me in the day of trouble. I will deliver thee, and thou shalt glorify Me.*

They had indeed called upon Him, and He had answered.

13

✳ The Besieged Castle ✳

AFTER THIS NARROW ESCAPE the chaplain advised that they remain concealed until later in the night than usual, for the queen was so exhausted from her unaccustomed exertion that she must have all the rest that could be obtained.

Her three companions had given her all the assistance possible. Hildeward and Hedwig had supported her on each side; Hildeward had even carried her in his strong arms over rough places and streams.

In the early dawn of morning they saw in the distance a body of water, which Martin recognized as the Mincio River, which runs close to Mantua, and was gratified that he had been successful in guiding them in the direction of Reggio.

In the dim light they saw a fisherman on the shore with his boat. Martin hurried to meet him, and asked his assistance.

After a short conversation he saw that he was a man that could be trusted, and he told him who they were, and where they intended to go.

"My cabin is on the other side," he said. "I will row you over, and there the poor young queen will be as safe as she can be anywhere upon earth."

The small river was narrow at that point, and soon they were in the little place, which was so hidden by trees and shrubbery that no one expected to find a dwelling there.

With flint and steel a fire was lighted and the fisherman,

quite an adept by reason of long practice, cooked the fresh fish over the coals, which, with brown bread, made a meal for the hungry travelers long to be remembered by them.

The bed, though hard, was a place of sweet rest to the weary queen. She remained in the hut most of the day, feeling a sense of security and peace to which she was a stranger in Garda Castle; and never, in all the luxury she enjoyed later on, did she forget the three peaceful days she passed in the fisherman's cottage. She thanked God, too, that He had given her four such noble friends in those dark hours of persecution.

She did not dare leave the seclusion of the cabin during the day, but when night came on, she and two of her faithful companions could enjoy the fresh, fragrant air of the forest.

The chaplain was on his way to Reggio. He had planned, as soon as the queen would be in a safe place, to go and see Bishop Adelard and ask him to send a company of soldiers to convey the queen to whatever place he considered safest. Dressed in his soldier suit, no one would for a moment take him for a priest.

The journey to Reggio was not without danger, and it required all his ingenuity to avoid meeting the emissaries of Berengarius. But he succeeded. Arriving at the palace of Bishop Adelard, he told of the escape of Queen Adelheid from Garda Castle and of her long, weary walk to see him and be under his protection.

The bishop was glad to learn the queen had escaped, and that he could help her. He immediately summoned a company of soldiers to go to the fisherman's cottage under the guidance of chaplain Martin, and take the queen and her attendants to Canossa Castle. He sent three horses along for the fugitives.

At the same time he sent a messenger to Steward Azzo, telling him of the queen's coming, asking him to have his soldiers armed and ready to meet the enemy in case of a surprise.

This request was promptly attended to, and soon everything was in readiness for the coming of the queen and her attendants.

When Martin and the soldiers reached the cabin, the queen sank upon her knees, and with uplifted hands and streaming eyes thanked God for all His goodness to her. The chaplain, Hedwig, and Hildeward knelt with her.

Knight Azzo and his soldiers were waiting to receive them, and he won the confidence of the queen at the first interview. He was a noble, whole-souled man, and, what was of great importance to her, was a trusted friend of the bishop.

It was with tears of gratitude that Adelheid parted from the fisherman. "I will not forget your goodness to me," she said, clasping his hand in farewell. "The time may come when I shall be able to repay your kindness in giving me shelter under your roof," a promise which she nobly kept in providing for him a competency for life.

As she had turned from the cabin to mount the horse provided for her, Hildeward had a word of farewell.

"Now that your Majesty is safely on your way and under strong protection, you will permit me to return to my German home. On my way I hope to meet his Majesty King Otto, and tell him that you received his message, and that you will be found at Castle Canossa."

"I have much to thank you for, my friend," replied Adelheid, taking" his hand, while tears were filling her eyes. "Tell your king that he has much to be proud of in having you for an assistant. I hope our parting will not be for all time. Farewell, my brave, kind friend. May it please God that we meet again!"

Hildeward clasped the chaplain in his arms as he bade him farewell. "I can never, never forget what you have done for my sister and myself; had it not been for you, we would still be prisoners in Garda Castle."

On a high, steep, rocky place was Castle Canossa, and Queen Adelheid believed that in that isolated place and under the protection of Steward Azzo she would be perfectly safe. But it was not entirely so. Berengarius was incensed at her escape from Garda Castle, and threatened Steward Azzo with severe punishment.

Knight Azzo laughed at this, and sent him a message

to the effect that upon the steep rock where Canossa was placed, she could never again fall into his tyrannical hands. The events of the last few days had followed so rapidly that Berengarius had not time to prepare for a great storming of the castle; but he knew that it was not provisioned for any great length of time, and if he could not take the place by force of weapons, he could subdue its inmates by starvation. He would try storming it first, and, if not successful, he would put a bar upon food being taken into the castle.

Now that the queen was comfortably placed, Hildeward cheerily left Canossa and turned northward to his old home, his heart thrilling with the pleasurable thought of again meeting his uncle Gozbert, and hearing of his experiences since they parted at Garda Castle.

He had been several days on the way when he met three young men evidently out on their late summer jaunt to see the world, and to his glad surprise he found one of them to be a friend whom he knew and loved. "Wido," he exclaimed, "do I really see my cousin Wido?"

"You are right. I am rejoiced to see you!" and they clasped hands cordially.

With Wido were Hengist and Keringer, whom Wido had introduced as the sons of Gerhard von Stein, the owner of Hartrun Castle. They were greatly surprised and highly pleased when Hildeward informed them that they, too, were his cousins.

"How did we become your cousins?" asked Keringer eagerly.

"Your father, Gerhard von Stein, and my father, Conrad von Stein, were brothers."

"Who told you of it?"

"Your uncle and mine, Uncle Gozbert, when I was with him in his cabin in the great forest of Merseburg. He is forester and hunter for King Otto."

"But how did he become our uncle?" asked Hengist.

"His sister was the wife of Gerhard von Stein; she was your mother. She was also the sister of Wido's father, Uncle Ruppert, for he and Uncle Gozbert are brothers, which makes Wido a cousin to all three of us. We four are first cousins."

There was another hearty shaking of hands over this happy relationship, and the cousins went to the shade of the trees on the edge of the forest and talked of things past and present.

"Now tell me," said Hildeward, "how it is that you three from the distant land of Saxony come into the hostile land of Italy at this time of change of rulers; for these war times are not without danger."

"I will tell you," said Wido. "The knowledge of the intention of King Otto to raise in all haste an army to get Queen Adelheid out of prison was not long in reaching Beleke and Hartrun castles. We heard that all the qualified soldiers rushed to the gathering-places, for a wonderful enthusiasm prevailed. How could we sit still in our homes? My father was willing that I should join the army of King Otto, for since the time of that great trouble between King Otto and his brother, Duke Henry of Bavaria, which ended in a complete reconciliation between the brothers, my father has abandoned all hatred against King Otto and his adherents. God be praised, he is entirely changed.

"At Regensburg we had the good fortune to see the mustering of the army. Besides the great army of footsoldiers, there were horsemen, knights, counts, princes, and barons, all full of enthusiasm. There was a company of footsoldiers with cross-bows and arrows, another company with slings, another with clubs, another with lances, and the horsemen were all in armor.

"The feudal vassals who gathered at the call of the king were now free men as a reward of faithful service in battle.

"The army was composed of well-drilled soldiers, who have been in many a feud, and though never having been on a battle-field, they know how to use the weapons.

"Some who wished to go into battle were not allowed, because they were not experienced in using the weapons, and knew nothing of the rules of warfare. Among those accepted are carpenters, butchers, hunters, fishermen, fowlers, who had been trained in the use of weapons. The handling of the clubs is an art, as is spear-throwing, the use of slings, which is really more of an art than the others, and footmen as well as horsemen can wheel and turn in an amazing manner.

"The king was charmed to see Hengist and Keringer," continued Wido. "He called them his young deliverers, having saved him not only from the teeth of the bear, but also from the stiletto of the assassin. He also gave me his hand and said that I, too, had been a deliverer of one of his House."

"When did the army leave for Italy?" asked Hildeward.

"The middle of September. They marched through the day and rested at night in their camps, the king's tent being in the middle. Now, cousin, you will have a chance to see King Otto and his army. As we reached the foot of the Alps over which the troops were to pass, the king called us to him and said, 'You boys can travel much faster than my army, and you may be able to reach Italian soil much earlier. Probably you can do me a service. I have sent two messengers to Garda Castle in Italy to tell the queen that I and my army intend to come to free her from prison, but have not as yet heard if she has received the message. It would be a great comfort to her to know that we are on the way. Perhaps you three boys may contrive some way to send her a letter from me.'

"Of course, we joyously answered that we would do the best we could, and he gave us a letter written by his own hand which we are to give to her if we can.

"We have crossed the Alps and have now reached Italy. We will lay aside our German traveling garb. Just as we crossed, we had a great surprise, for we came unexpectedly upon a company of Swabian soldiers of Duke Ludolph of Swabia, the son of King Otto. He had secretly gone to Italy to free Queen Adelheid before King Otto could get here, and as yet the king knows nothing of this undertaking."

"God be praised!" said Hildeward reverently, "that I have heard something of Ludolph. But I fear it will be displeasing to the king, and no good will come of it. The duke should not have gone on that venture."

"Where is Queen Adelheid?" asked Wido.

"She is in Canossa Castle," said Hildeward, and he told them the whole story of being sent, accompanied by Uncle Gozbert, to try to get a message to the queen, and how it was done, to which the cousins listened with intense interest.

"Now I fear," he added, "that Berengarius will get news of the coming of Prince Ludolph, and it will harm the cause of the queen. No doubt, Uncle Gozbert is with the prince, so I need not search for him. Now, cousins," he continued, "I must keep on my way to meet the king, and tell him of the result of my commission to the queen."

"We, too, will keep on our way, and we are certainly happy to have met you, and to have received so much information."

The four cousins clasped hands in farewell, and Hildeward continued his course northward, while the three kept on the way pointed out by him to Canossa Castle.

Steadily they walked for several days, only halting to rest and eat their simple food. At length the castle came in view. It was surrounded by Berengarius' soldiery, just what Hildeward told them they might expect. The king was with his soldiers, so eager was he to have the queen again a prisoner in his hands.

The three emissaries of King Otto, under the protection of their German clothes, watched the movements of the besiegers with alert interest, especially their efforts to make the siege batteries do the work expected of them.

But this they could not do; the projectile machines could throw the stones only to the foot of the rock upon which stood the castle, not even reaching to the foundation of the great building.

Foiled in this attempt of storming the place, Berengarius resolved to allow no food to be carried in to the prisoners; he would starve them into submission.

The three boys almost lost hope of being able to give the message of King Otto to Queen Adelheid. At length a thought came to Wido of how it might be done, which was to send the letter by means of cross-bow and arrow.

"But where would you aim, not knowing the apartment occupied by the queen?" asked Hengist.

"I believe that anyone who sees the letter with the king's seal upon it will know that it will be wise to deliver it to the queen or into the hands of the steward, who is her friend and protector."

"You are right. How stupid of us not to have thought of it at once! We have wasted time and perhaps attracted the attention of the enemy. The arrow might have been sent up without being noticed by anyone. But where will you get a bow and arrow?"

"I thought of walking with one of the soldiers this evening. That will give me an opportunity to notice where in the camp I can best secure them, and from that point I will see which is the best place to take my aim."

"You are running some risk," said Keringer, "and you are showing great bravery in thinking of carrying out this really ingenious plan. I believe you will succeed."

That evening Wido secured a bow and arrow, and fastening the king's letter to the queen to the point of the arrow, he shot it straight through the window at which it was aimed.

In the meantime the inmates of the castle were suffering from want of food. Azzo had done his best to give them aid; even the domestic animals had been slain to satisfy the pangs of hunger.

Daily he looked out of the windows to see if King Otto's troops were in view, but noticed no signs of their coming.

Adelheid and Hedwig were among the sufferers. They saw the need in the castle was growing greater day by day, and that the steward had no words of comfort. Doubt, indeed, filled the hearts of every one at the castle that the troops would reach there before it would be too late.

Had some disaster hindered the king's coming or had he changed his mind" was a question that no one could answer.

To be so weak from hunger that the body trembled was hard enough for strong men to bear, but that the gentle, lovely young queen should suffer for want of suitable food filled Azzo with distress, while the queen urged that because of her others should not suffer.

How to save the queen from the tyranny of Berengarius was Azzo's one thought. The hosts of soldiers that surrounded the castle made escape impossible. There was no subterranean passageway as in many other castles, nor a secret stairway leading to the open.

On the morning of the third day there was great excitement among the soldiers in the courtyard. One of them had found an arrow on the roof of a horse-stall, and fastened securely to its point was a parchment sealed with the seal of King Otto.

Without delay Steward Azzo opened it, but as address and letter were in a foreign language, which he believed to be German, he took it to Queen Adelheid with haste.

"God be praised!" she exclaimed. "Help is near. King Otto is coming; indeed, he is very near. When need is greatest, then God's help is nearest."

The next morning the castle and surroundings reëchoed with the news that Berengarius had called off the siege, and that the great German emperor King Otto was approaching with a large army to save the queen. In less than an hour the place was clear of Berengarius' soldiers.

King Otto was accompanied by his brother, Duke Henry of Bavaria, Duke Conrad of Lothringia, and others of the nobility. He had in good time met Hildeward, who had told him where the queen was to be found, also of the threatened siege. The troops were then put to a forced march.

On the way the king met Prince Ludolph with his small army. He was incensed at his foolish undertaking, and rebuked him severely, as did his Uncle Henry of Bavaria, who scoffed with such contemptuous raillery that his treatment was bitterly resented.

"The king has a right to reproach me," Ludolph said, "because he is my father. But in no way is it your duty to reprimand me as if I were but a boy under your care. You would have more reason to think of your own misdeeds, and especially the one against my father's life."

To this Duke Henry angrily responded, whereupon he heard some more remarks which were not at all complimentary, and they parted, anything but good friends.

Instead of the laurels he expected to win, Ludolph had met only reproach and ridicule. Ashamed of the whole affair, he deeply regretted that he had not taken the advice of Hildeward and never set out on the wild attempt to free the queen.

At Pavia the king halted with his army, and sent a company of his most distinguished men to Canossa with costly presents to the queen, and asked her hand in marriage.

Adelheid was greatly surprised, but expressed her willingness to become the king's wife, and be under the protection of the ruler of Germany. She had never seen him, but had heard much praise as to his appearance and nobility of character.

The messengers who had brought the presents and offer of marriage to the queen were instructed to bring her to Pavia, where the king kept court, and where he would await her coming.

Accompanied by Hedwig and Chaplain Martin, as well as many brave knights and soldiers, Adelheid left Canossa Castle for Pavia. It was a triumphal journey. The people came in crowds to see her, the young and beautiful queen, who had passed through such frightful experiences. "Long life to our beautiful Queen Adelheid!" was the cry of joyous enthusiasm; for she was loved by the people while Berengarius was hated.

More than half way on the journey to Pavia they were met by Duke Henry of Bavaria, who was appointed by the king to give her his greeting, and he was followed by a retinue of stately horsemen to escort her to Pavia.

Duke Henry was so cordial, and evinced such brotherly kindness, that Adelheid never in after life forgot it, but had a real sisterly affection for him, of which he was truly worthy; for since the time of his terrible conspiracy against King Otto and the sincere and hearty forgiveness granted him by his brother, he was a changed man.

In Pavia, the main city of Berengarius, the people were eagerly expecting the queen. Thousands of the citizens upon splendid horses, and musicians with trumpets, kettledrums, and cymbals, passed through the main streets following the royal cortege. Upon the balconies were richly dressed ladies, waving their greetings to the lovely young queen.

Although King Otto had heard much of her beauty, he was in no way disappointed in her appearance, and her sweet, gentle manner won his heart, while she was equally pleased with the stately, majestic appearance and the expression of goodness upon the handsome features of her future husband.

In the autumn of the year 951 was celebrated with great splendor the marriage of King Otto of Germany and Queen Adelheid of Italy, in the populous city of Pavia, where the queen, a little over a year before, had suffered such anguish of mind.

Distinguished guests from Germany and Italy traveled long distances to attend the wedding festivities. Food for thousands had to be provided, not only for the guests, but also for a great number of horses.

The banners of the nobility and the shields of the knights added to the gay appearance of the palace, and in the streets there were not only the guests, but also traveling people who came of their own free will. Minstrels, acrobats, and like entertainers were there in great numbers, reaping a rich harvest during the three days of the festivities.

Never to be forgotten was the pageant of the royal bridal pair to the church, and when the archbishop put the king's ring upon the finger of Adelheid and pronounced the blessing, she could not but compare the present with the sad times through which she had passed.

In a corner of the church, where they had a full view of the service, were Hedwig and Martin, Uncle Gozbert, and the four cousins. Tears of joy were in the eyes of the two who had shared the two prisons with the happy bride.

Great preparations were made for the tables at which the people were to be feasted. Herds of cattle, deer, and fowls were killed, and the whole three days were to the people of Pavia a time of jollity and good cheer, never to be forgotten.

14

❧ Rebellion against King Otto ❧

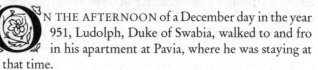N THE AFTERNOON of a December day in the year 951, Ludolph, Duke of Swabia, walked to and fro in his apartment at Pavia, where he was staying at that time.

At a window sat Hildeward, gazing at the beautiful landscape without, but with unseeing eyes. The garden and grounds of King Otto's palace which a few weeks before had been gay and fragrant, were now covered with snow, and the shrubbery and trees in their white covering were beautiful under the beams of the afternoon sun.

Hildeward's thoughts, however, were not upon the scenery, but upon the troubles of the young prince Ludolph, and his faithful heart was sad.

"You may say what you will, Hildeward," said Ludolph, without pausing in his walk, "but there is no one who disturbs my peace as does my uncle, Duke Henry. Anyone can see that he is doing his best to turn my father against me, or at least weaken his affection for me, and I cannot see how it is that my father and you are so blinded."

"I see all, your Highness, because my position in palace and castle gives me the opportunity to know that you are not friendly to him."

"Why should I make a secret of it? To me it seems incredible that, after doing his best to assassinate my father, he can now evince such devotion and loyalty to him; not openly and honorably, as a brother should, but by cajoling and wheedling like a subservient menial."

"You go too far in your censure, my prince, to speak that way of the duke; instead of censuring him, you ought to see that he is doing his best to make amends for the terrible crime which he intended to commit, as we know and all the world knows; and the shame and remorse must be hard for him to endure. Would it not be better to help him forget what causes him anguish every time he thinks of it?"

"But see how he has treated me! Had I been left to carry out my plans in freeing Queen Adelheid from prison, it would have been done, and my father and his army would have been spared the hardship of crossing the Alps. He, Uncle Henry, circumvented me by sending messengers to the cities; and when I reached Italy, the gates of the Italian cities were closed against me as though I were an enemy. Just think of my humiliation! I, the only heir to the throne of Germany! — and all the fault of Uncle Henry."

Hildeward did not make reply to this. He deeply sympathized with the prince, but would not add fuel to the flame by censuring Duke Henry.

"If it were not to his advantage, you would not see so much adulation and toadyism," continued Ludolph. "Believe me, it was not my father's choice that Uncle Henry went in King Otto's name to receive Queen Adelheid as she came from Canossa to Pavia. His thirst for honor made him press himself into this service of welcoming her, and through it he won the friendship of the queen and the gratitude of my father. This he has done, and in doing so, he usurped the place which by right was mine as heir to the crown; or if not to me, the honor of welcoming the queen should have been given my sister's husband, Conrad, Duke of Lothringia. No! it must be Uncle Henry; and through him we were pushed into the background."

"The queen's noble heart and the king's sense of justice will not allow your Highness nor Duke Conrad to suffer neglect for anyone; both are worthy of your highest respect and love."

"Had it not been for my uncle's malicious interference, I would have had the triumph of releasing Queen Adelheid from prison. He set the most eminent among the Italians against me, and the gates were closed to me, which made me a target for the jeers of the people, who believed me to be a foolish, reckless idiot. How can I do else than hate him?"

"You are in a fair way to have not only a bitter enemy in your uncle, but also to anger your father. Oh, my prince, reflect before you say or do something you will greatly regret! Forget the mistake you made in trying to free the queen. Your intention was good, and if it proved a failure, it is not the only failure that has been made, and by older and more experienced men than yourself."

"I could not bear enmity against my father," said Ludolph; "my love for him is too deep. I would not battle against him, but against Duke Henry. However, if my father persists, as he has done, in setting me aside for his brother, what else can I do, no matter how painful it may be, than to turn my weapons against him?"

"You surely would not do that?" exclaimed Hildeward in pained astonishment.

"Not unless it were necessary. I cannot remain peaceful while my uncle is trying to estrange my father and the queen from me. He would cast me entirely aside, and endanger my right to the crown of Germany. So I intend to leave Pavia tomorrow morning for Germany. It is useless and foolish for me to remain here. I have always willingly listened to your advice, and never took offense at what you said, but this time I will not follow it. I will give you an hour to decide whether you will stay with me or with my father. I also ask you to promise me that you will not impart this confidential conversation to anyone. Will you do it? If so, shake hands."

"I promise," said Hildeward, and clasped the hand of the one he loved so much, and with whom he sympathized so sincerely in his humiliated and depressed condition, as well as because of the influence Duke Henry had gained over the king, who had opened his whole heart to him and had given him his protection, as if he had never conspired against him.

On the other hand, Hildeward also sympathized with King Otto, who had shown his love for his son Ludolph in every way, already when but a boy, bestowing upon him the Grand Duchy of Swabia, and assuring him the succession to the throne of Germany. He knew also that King Otto was innocent of any intention of causing his son to have reason for disliking Duke Henry.

In great perplexity the young man stood at the window and reflected what were best for him to do. He finally decided to go to the monastery of Honoldsheim, instead of to his Uncle Gozbert, to whom he had first thought of going; but the quiet, monotonous life in the cabin in the forest, while welcome at some times in his life, was not what he needed. He longed for the companionship of Chaplain Martin, that dear friend of the dark days at Garda Castle, and resolved to go to him.

Queen Adelheid's first thought after her marriage was to show her gratitude to those who had been her faithful friends in adversity.

To Martin she gave what she knew would give the greatest happiness, the position of abbot in the wealthy monastery at Honoldsheim, in Bavaria. Upon Knight Azzo she bestowed the title of count, and made him a member of the Counts of the German Empire. King Otto rewarded others for their faithfulness to her later. Knowing that he would be gladly welcomed by Martin, Hildeward's unrest was quelled at the thought of being with him, and his spirits rose accordingly.

The next morning Ludolph left Pavia quietly. His leaving the city was not known to King Otto for two days, when he sent for Hildeward to find out the cause of his departure.

At the last meeting of father and son there was coldness and restraint instead of the former congenial companionship. King Otto did not understand the change, and hoped that Hildeward could give him some light on the subject.

Hildeward felt it an unpleasant duty to tell him what he knew, but as tenderly as possible he imparted to him his own opinion without breaking his promise to Ludolph.

"I think Prince Ludolph feels that you show more affection for your brother, the Duke of Bavaria, than for him, your Majesty," said Hildeward, "and he feels that his Highness Duke Henry does not show him the consideration and respect which is due him as your son and heir to the throne;

especially does he feel this in respect to the Duke's severe censure for the mistake he made in going to Italy to release her Majesty the Queen from prison, a mistake which causes him much humiliation."

Hildeward had intended to go directly to the monastery at Honoldsheim, but about the time of the Christmas festival a report spread over Germany that Duke Ludolph had called together the representative men of the kingdom at Saalfeld to lay before them his grievances against Duke Henry and, because of him, against King Otto, his brother's protector and defender.

The report was not long in reaching the king, and he groaned in the depths of his heart upon hearing it.

"Can it be really the will of God that this trouble has come upon me through my nearest and dearest kin?" he said mournfully. "First my brother, whom I loved and favored, sought to take my life and cause me hours of grief, and now my son, whom I dearly loved, due to misunderstandings, and from want of confidence in me, takes up arms against me. Oh, merciful God, spare me this bitter trouble! But not my will, but Thine be done. In all my troubles, Thou hast hitherto stood by me."

As was natural to King Otto, he bore this new heavy grief with Christian resignation and even with serenity. He summoned his son-in-law, Duke Conrad of Lorraine, who showed his usual cordial, friendly manner, so that the king had no thought that this same son-in-law was on the point of joining the rebellion against him.

Duke Conrad was a tall, strong man and a brave, resolute, determined soldier, and there was no prince who could compare with him in appearance and as to his renowned qualities as a soldier. Not only was he master of the use of the sword, and all other weapons of the time, but as a leader in battle he had no superior.

"It is sad news that has come to me from Germany," said the king when Duke Conrad stood before him. "It may be my good fortune to extinguish the torch that my son Ludolph has lighted. I had hoped to stay in Italy to punish Berengarius, and also to unwind the intrigue which is preventing the pope from giving me one of the great wishes of my heart, to be crowned a Caesar at Rome, as was my great predecessor, Charlemagne. But the danger beyond the Alps is too great for me to remain here. I know from experience what a small affair will bring on a war in my kingdom, and I must be there to nip it in the bud. May the Almighty be with me in the effort! I wish you, my dear Conrad, to take my place here in Italy and uphold my cause. It will require strength to do this, and I feel confident that you will use it."

Conrad expressed entire willingness to undertake the task. But notwithstanding all the energy and excellent management, King Otto was not ready to leave Italy until the early part of February. Then, accompanied by Queen Adelheid, Duke Henry of Bavaria, and a company of soldiers, they left Pavia, and it was Easter before they reached Saxony, where they were greeted with enthusiasm, the beautiful and gracious queen being beloved by all.

As the dew disappears under the beams of the sun, so the presence of the royal husband and wife quelled all disturbance.

The matchless personality of the king, his serenity of manner and apparent obliviousness of any disturbance, soothed the public mind as nothing else could have done, and all trouble was forgotten with the disappearance of rebellion against lawful authority.

In the meantime the affairs in Italy were not so pleasant as King Otto desired. Scarcely had he departed for Germany, when Berengarius began to usurp authority.

He vigorously sought adherents to assist him in getting the possession and holding the castles and fortresses, that he might take the field against Duke Conrad of Lorraine.

They battled, and the brave Duke soon vanquished his antagonist, and advised him to go to Germany and see the king, who was at Magdeburg and own submission to him, assuring him of a kind reception.

Berengarius took the advice. But when he presented himself to King Otto, he met with such scornful severity that he was incensed, as was also Duke Conrad, who had pledged his word for a kind reception and had accompanied him to Magdeburg.

Angry disdain was shown Berengarius by King Otto because he suspected him of being the cause of the death of King Lothair, as well as because of his inhuman treatment of Queen Adelheid, and his persistence in calling himself King of Italy.

Duke Conrad laid the blame of the whole affair upon Duke Henry, whom he suspected of turning his father-in-law, King Otto, against him, as did Ludolph; and Duke Henry, angered at both, prevented a reconciliation with the king.

Ludolph had another trouble that was weighing on his mind; a son had been born to the royal pair, and he feared that a son of the beloved Adelheid would exclude him from the throne.

15

✢ The Hungarians Again ✢

FOUR YEARS HAD PASSED, and three of those years had been passed happily by Hildeward in the monastery of Honoldsheim, where he was busily engaged in good works for the poor and ailing, and for every one who needed help, as well as in his duties in the school.

One pleasant summer evening, in the year 955, he was waiting for the return of Abbot Martin, who had been to Freising in Bavaria, and was expected back that day.

Hildeward was eager to see him, and to know what he had seen and heard, for in the secluded monastery, news of the outside world was precious.

At length he could not restrain the wish to go to meet him, and, mounting his horse, he set out on the rough road to Freising. He had not traveled far, when he saw in the distance a small cavalcade of horsemen; and he recognized the leader as Abbot Martin, his sword by his side, and guarded by four servants with chain armors, helmets, swords, spears, and daggers. Hildeward's eyes brightened with joy at seeing his dear friend.

"Thank God that you have reached home safely, Father Martin," he said, wheeling about to ride beside him, and they clasped hands in cordial greeting.

"It is good in you to come to meet me, Hildeward. Is all going on well in Honoldsheim?"

"All's well, as usual. But we certainly missed our dear good abbot, and are glad to welcome you back. Did you enjoy your outing?"

"Yes, in a way; yet the eight days of my visit seemed as so many weeks."

"Are you bringing any news of Augsburg?"

"Not altogether new," and a shadow passed over Martin's noble features. "What we have heard in our secluded home in the monastery is only an echo of the proceedings."

"I was so anxious to see you and know what was going on in Bavaria that I could not wait until you reached the monastery, and so went to meet you. But I see that you are pale and weary from your journey, and I will not question you until you have had some refreshment."

"Ever thoughtful, my dear Hildeward. The towers of our dear Benedictine monastery of Honoldsheim are in full sight; we will soon be there, and my short absence from it has made me appreciate more than ever my native place, my Honoldsheim, and its villagers. I hope the pupils of our school gave you no trouble?"

"No; all went along smoothly. I had not the least trouble with the pupils."

The abbot and Hildeward conducted a large school in the monastery. All branches of learning and industry were taught. The abbot, in his early years, before becoming chaplain at Garda Castle, had been a valued teacher in the neighborhood, and was loved by all.

When they had reached the cloister, Hildeward had a servant bring a refreshing meal to the weary abbot. When the abbot had finished his meal and was somewhat rested, he related to Hildeward what he had seen and heard, which was all new to him, although it had happened months before.

"King Otto and Queen Adelheid celebrated their Christmas festivities at Frankfort-on-the-Main, and shortly after Easter they went to Engelheim, the castle of Duke Henry of Bavaria, who had gone there several days before to make due preparations for the royal visitors.

"But the king and queen did not remain long, for there was trouble brewing secretly. From different sources the report reached the king that there were gatherings in the castles of Duke Ludolph and Duke Conrad, and that they were making preparations for battle. The gathering was composed of the daring, reckless young men of Franconia, Saxony, and Bavaria.

"This matter caused King Otto unspeakable distress, and again and again he said, 'Can it be possible that my own son would turn against me with the weapons of war?'

"'We are not safe here,' he said to Queen Adelheid. 'We will go to Mayence, where we will feel more secure.'

"His brother Henry agreed with him, and for his own safety, they decided to return to Saxony. So the three left Engelheim Castle at the same time.

"The king sent a message to Mayence announcing his coming, and expected that the gates of the fortified city would be opened to him, and that he and the queen would be received by the citizens with loyal affection. But he was bitterly disappointed; the gates were closed, and no citizens came to receive him.

"After a little while the strong iron-bound gate swung open, and the king, queen and their attendants passed in. Now the king learned the cause of the delay. The adherents of Dukes Conrad and Ludolph were busy with their war preparations and had made as speedy an exit as possible. They did not consider their insurrection as being leveled against the king, but against Duke Henry, as there was a feud between them and him which they had sworn to settle by force of arms.

"Adelheid was like a comforting angel in this dark hour.

"The king decided to sail on the Rhine to Cologne and visit his mother at Dortmund, the pious and clear-headed Queen Matilda. Here, with his beloved wife and mother, King Otto passed a restful time. Under the roof of his mother's castle, and thanks to her sagacious counsel, he came to a clear understanding of the state of affairs. He regained his composure and self-reliance, and looked upon the future with manly serenity.

"Filled with new courage, he declared the Mayence League null and void, threatened to take the dukedoms from Conrad and Ludolph, and outlaw them by putting the ban of the kingdom upon them.

"Ludolph and Conrad believed this to be nothing more than an empty threat, and paid no attention to it. But the king called a parliament at Fritzlar to consider the question of the insurrection.

"He did this without delay, for the report came to him that the affair of waging war against him had not been given up; on the contrary, the dukes were near at hand, having gained the needed assistance. Especially Duke Conrad had greatly strengthened his forces, and could scarcely be expected to wait.

"Dukes Conrad and Ludolph, though summoned to parliament, resolved not to go, but to proceed in their determination to make war upon the king. When parliament met, it decided against Duke Conrad, and the whole of Lothringia was with it.

"Duke Conrad hurried to Lothringia, thinking it would be but a trifle to bring all his adherents again to his side. Instead, he found himself bitterly mistaken; his own people had turned against him in fierce, bloody war. He was an outlaw, the ban of the kingdom being upon him.

"In sincere repentance he and Ludolph realized the foolishness of their rebellion and threw themselves upon their knees before King Otto, the only favor asked of him being that the friends and adherents who stood by them might not suffer punishment, and that they themselves might retain their dukedoms.

"But this the king would not grant. Ludolph and Conrad believed, and not without cause, that Duke Henry influenced the king against them."

"Oh, if Prince Ludolph had been blessed with a good advisor, whose warnings he would have taken!" said Hildeward, as Abbot Martin paused in his narration of events.

"He had the wisest and best of advisors, but he was too full of anger against his uncle Henry to take advice from anyone. King Otto's younger brother, the Archbishop of Brun, laid his hand upon Ludolph's shoulder and in kind, gentle words sought to soothe the angry prince.

"'Why, my dear nephew,' he said, 'have you brought all this trouble upon your father? Have you not noticed that his hair is turning gray before the usual time? You sin against God by not honoring your father. Not to your friends, but to your enemies you go for advice. They pretend to guide you, but they lead you astray. Once you were the pride of your father, the hope and promise of the whole kingdom. Think of his sighs — tears even — over your rebellion against him! Yet his heart is open and ready to receive his son, and he would rejoice over his return. He will again receive you with a loving heart, and in time will forgive your adherents. Oh, Ludolph, turn again to your father, love him as you once did, and that love will be returned in double measure.'

"Ludolph listened, but his heart was too full of bitter hatred and revenge against Duke Henry, whom he blamed for all his trouble, to take the advice to heart at that time.

"He and Conrad had headed with the king to pardon their adherents," continued Abbot Martin.

"'We are ready, father, Conrad and I, to take all the punishment you think we deserve,' said Ludolph with trembling lips and tear-dimmed eyes, 'but we ask for pardon for the poor men whom we drew into this trouble, which we sincerely regret.'"

"'That is just what one would expect of the noble young prince,' remarked Hildeward.

"'It is impossible for me to do this,' replied the king. 'How can I break my royal word and pardon the traitors who have taken up the sword against me?'"

"'Then, father, the war must go on,' said Ludolph; 'we have bound ourselves by oath not to accept pardon from you unless it were also granted to them. Hear our petition for them, father, and we will lay down our arms, never again to take them up against you.'"

"'Mercy and pardon for our friends,' implored Conrad."

"'I cannot, I dare not,' said the king, deeply moved; 'it would but open the way for further insurrections. This uprising, which was too weak to stand upon its feet, would grow stronger if not prevented. I have pardoned you and Conrad; I can do no more.'"

"He was right," commented Hildeward; "but what a severe trial for father and son!"

"Like fuel to the flame," continued Abbot Martin, "were the words of Duke Henry to Ludolph.

"'What was your object in battling against your father?' he asked. 'If you wished to battle with me, why not battle with me alone? Do you suppose I care anything for your enmity? Not so much as a blade of grass,' and he took one up, broke it, and threw it back. 'But what have you against your father, to make trouble for him? If your head and heart are in the right place, put your spite on me. I am not in the least afraid of you.'"

"Shameful of Duke Henry to speak that way to the troubled boy," commented Hildeward. "Strange that he does not think of his own deeds against King Otto."

"It is stranger still that Ludolph made no reply; he turned his back upon his uncle and walked away, followed by Duke Conrad. In his heart he knew that his uncle's influence with King Otto had prevented a reconciliation.

"The two former owners of dukedoms returned to Mayence," continued Abbot Martin, "and in Bavaria there was an open insurrection against Duke Henry, the former ruler. King Otto had to see that counts and barons were leaving his army and going over to the enemy, and the weight of grief and sorrow upon his troubled mind was increased. He and Duke Henry must battle with the insurgents not only on the Rhine, but on the Danube.

"The gates of Regensburg were opened to Ludolph and his soldiers, and he drove out the wife and child of his hated uncle Henry and took possession of the treasures of the dukedom. He did not keep them for himself, however, but distributed them among the soldiers as prizes. For six weeks the battle lasted; then he returned to Swabia.

"All the Bavarians were now turned against the king, and his position was full of danger. But he never lost courage; his trust and faith in God were his support in all the troubles of life; he returned to Saxony, and after a little delay Ludolph followed.

"The words of advice and entreaty of the archbishop had not been without effect. Ludolph's proud spirit was subdued, and he longed to be at peace with his father.

"With bare feet, as a penitent, he threw himself upon his knees and implored forgiveness.

"'Stand up, my son,' said the king, with tears in his kind eyes; 'you have given me much trouble, but I consider the circumstances that influenced you. I freely forgive you, but I cannot restore to you your dukedom, nor can I remove the ban of the empire until the next meeting of parliament which will not meet at Fritzlar, in December, but at Arnstadt, in Thuringia.'

"'I will give you and Conrad, who also asked my forgiveness, the castles you have owned, and Mayence. You will have the property in Swabia which you owned, and Conrad will have again in his possession his property in Franconia, but the dukedoms you and Conrad have lost for all time.'"

"The city of Mayence," remarked Hildeward, "would certainly be a safe place for anyone that wished protection from an enemy; with the high, strong walls surrounding it, its foundation deep in the earth, such a stronghold would be almost impregnable. To attack it with projectiles would be a senseless business; and it would be impossible to undermine it on account of its deep and solid foundations. Thousands of soldiers would be required to carry away the earth. The besieged would soon realize what was being done, and spears, arrows, and stones would be hurled down upon them and stop the work."

"Yes," said Abbot Martin; "and it is a joy to know that the unnatural war between father and son is ended, for it caused both great loss and sorrow."

It was a great pleasure in Hildeward's secluded life to learn all this from the lips of Abbot Martin; it gave him food for thought, and in his heart he pitied and sympathized at the same time; he pitied young Ludolph, who was tyrannized by Duke Henry; and he sympathized with the king, who so loved his son, but must not weaken in his authority over him.

⤚ ✳ ⤙

King Otto had scarcely reached Saxony, when he received a message from the Hungarians, which at first sight might have been considered friendly, for it was worded: *We are coming to the greatest king upon earth, the sun among the stars, to acknowledge our yielding to his majesty, and to admire him face to face.*

But Otto was quick to perceive the cunning flattery in these words. The Hungarians wanted to inspect the German lands, and see if it were possible to invade them. Otto, however, acted as though he did not perceive their real motive, but gave the messenger a liberal compensation.

Scarcely had the man departed when a message came from Duke Henry that the Hungarians had entered the southern part of Germany, and were spreading over it like an impetuous river — at least a hundred thousand strong.

"They will fight us now," continued Duke Henry's message, "for the reason that we are in such confusion owing to our own battles and troubles, and are still bleeding from the wounds we received. They boast that their horses will drink our German rivers dry, and their hoofs will stamp out our cities, and we will be trodden down with such force that we will forget to rise, and for all time will be their slaves."

"Truly, this disaster is too much for meek man to bear," said King Otto sadly, "but God reigns supreme. He will be with me, and grant me victory."

The case did seem almost hopeless. The king had but a small army to meet the enemy, and some sagacious, faithful men must be sent to the southern part of the kingdom to see how matters really stood. These faithful ones were Steward Ruppert, of Beleke Castle, and his son Wido, and Hengist and Keringer, sons of Gerhard von Stein.

Ruppert, in the years which had passed, had grown gray, but like a giant he sat upon his powerful horse, his gray eyes beaming with pleasure because he had been chosen to go on such an important expedition.

A helmet was on his head, a red shield hung by a leather hand from his shoulder, and his sword was at his side. The three younger men were also well armed.

"How is it now with your father?" asked the king of the young men from Hartrun Castle; "he is now well advanced in years."

"Yes, your Majesty, he is now nearly eighty, but still strong and in good health and enjoys the hunt. The fine chestnut horse you gave him is somewhat stiff, but is still eager for the hunt. My father would be delighted to go on this expedition," added Keringer.

"He is doing his share in sending his two sons; that is indeed self-denial," commented the king.

"You were once against me, old friend," continued Otto, turning with a smile to Ruppert, "but I rejoice to see that now you are on my side."

"Yes, I will now make good. Your noble treatment of my loved benefactor, Duke Henry, melted the ice about my heart; now I am a faithful servant and adherent of your Majesty."

"But I fear that you will be exposed to great danger from these wild, reckless invaders. Perhaps at your age it would be better for you to remain in your quiet home."

"The burden of years will not keep me from doing all I can. I could not stay at home when our kingdom is in danger."

"I am sure that you will do your duty. How many winters have come and gone for you?"

"One and seventy, gracious king; and in spite of my gray beard I hope to see some of the pagan visitors have reason to be sorry they came."

"You will surely be the oldest soldier in my company; and I am proud to have you."

"With your permission, gracious king, I would like to tell you that my brother Gozbert, your forester and hunter, would be glad to go with us if he were told of this danger to our fatherland; he would much rather be a soldier than a hunter."

"I know Gozbert well, and know that he will fight with great valor for me and for our kingdom. He has stood on the battle-field with me and was brave and efficient. I have heard that he has gone to be with his nephew Hildeward in the monastery at Honoldsheim."

This report was correct. Gozbert had yearned for the company of his beloved nephew Hildeward, and, several months ago, had left his solitary cabin in the forest and walked to the Honoldsheim monastery. Hildeward had welcomed him with open arms, and Abbot Martin had received him with heartfelt pleasure. In that secluded place they had heard nothing' of the invasion of the Hungarians.

One of the many duties that Hildeward had taken upon himself at the monastery was the providing of wild game for the table, a charge of which Gozbert took delight in relieving him.

In the great forest were the hiding-places of deer and other wild game, and uncle and nephew knew these places by instinct, and never failed in securing all that was needed.

One morning they were surprised to see several horsemen, clad in the skins of animals, small men with long hair, well armed with bows and arrows, spears and slings, and their speech strange to the two hunters.

"They are Huns," whispered Gozbert. "God grant that a wild horde of them are not again in our land! Wicked, ferocious robbers they are. These are scouts and spies, come to see where to make an attack."

"We must not lose a moment's time in warning the people at the monastery that they make speedy flight," said Hildeward anxiously.

"But let us first settle with these spies for all time," said Gozbert, the fire of the soldier lighting his eyes.

"No, uncle; it will not do to attack them. One thrust of a spear or a stone from a sling would finish you or me. And see, hanging from each saddle there is a noose, which they throw, never missing their aim, then plunge away on their swift horses, dragging the poor body after them until life is crushed out."

On the well-known path Hildeward led the way to the monastery, and the information gave much alarm and caused intense excitement. Some of the monks remembered a former invasion of the Huns, the barbarians climbing the walls and obtaining entrance. They were in the power of the invaders, who robbed the place of its treasures, plundered the cellar by taking all the eatables with them, and on leaving, threw a firebrand into the building.

Abbot Martin and all the inmates of the monastery realized the danger, but knew not what course to take to protect themselves.

"Pack the best of your possessions and resort to flight," said Gozbert. "I will drive the cattle into the forest, and leave all the doors open; for when those yellow rascals see the place abandoned, they will think there is nothing left worth stealing, and these wild horsemen have no inclination to remain long in a place where there is no booty to carry away."

"You are right in all points," said the abbot in his serene manner; "we will hasten to one of our castles, where we will find shelter and protection, and as soon as the Huns scurry through this region, we will return." Saying this, he set out with Hildeward.

Three of the monks took care of the Moorish tapestry, and others secured other valuable things for safe-keeping. With heavy hearts they took up the line of march, not knowing if their home would be as they left it or a mass of smoking ruins when they would return.

Gozbert joined them in the forest, and went with them to the castle, where Abbot Martin and his flock were heartily welcomed, and would be sheltered and protected. Then uncle and nephew kept on their way to Augsburg, for it would be in the richest city of the empire that the Huns would be likely to make their depredations, no longer scattered bands, but a great organized army, determined to conquer Germany.

In the neighborhood of Freising uncle and nephew saw with anxiety a company of Hungarian soldiers, and with difficulty avoided them. With them were the same scouts that they had seen in the forest.

The city of Freising had nothing to attract their greed, and in a spirit of destruction they set it on fire. The little town went up in flames and smoke.

On the way the two horsemen saw bodies of the country people who had been ruthlessly slain, their weapons still in their hands, and the wild horde had swept on to Augsburg.

16

❦ The Battle of Augsburg ❧

N THE CITY OF AUGSBURG the Huns expected to meet with but little resistance; for although a populous city, the walls surrounding it were not high, and towers could be dispensed with. But it was of no benefit to the defenders that the people of the surrounding country fled to the city with their goods for safety and protection; they were in their way.

The leader of the defense was the brave and pious Bishop Adalrich, a true friend of King Otto. He had been the guest of the king, and had accompanied him on hunts in the forest where Gozbert, as hunter and forester, had seen him and admired him greatly.

They had scarcely reached Augsburg, when the Huns appeared, swooping over the city like an immense dark swarm of grasshoppers. The blowing of trumpets, the clashing of cymbals, and other wild music, not pleasant to the ear, announced their coming to the citizens.

On some of the horses of the wild horde were utensils used in the celebration of the mass, and richly embroidered covers, by which one could rightly judge that the robbers had been through the monastery and had carried off all that pleased their fancy.

In advance of the great army was the leader, Bulzu, "Prince of the Princes." On his head was a helmet with an eagle with outspread wings, and on each side of his face hung locks of long hair. He was the indisputable master of horsemanship; his arrow never failed to pierce a bird on the wing, and with his curved saber he could without fail sever the head from the body of an enemy.

"We should meet the enemy outside, and not allow them to enter," said the leader of the German force to Bishop Adalrich.

"That would be a bad beginning," replied the bishop serenely. The words were scarcely uttered when the doors of the walled city were broken in, and the Huns were swarming through the streets.

The bishop met them in his official robes, without helmet or coat of mail. Arrows and stones from the slings flew about him like hail, but he remained calm. Near him were Gozbert and Hildeward, two warriors whose one thought was that of protecting him. Many a deadly missile aimed at him was warded off by their shields, and many a Hun who, with spear in hand, ran to him, was struck down by Gozbert's or Hildeward's sword.

It was a fierce battle, and the Huns filled the air with howls and shrieks as they took to flight, leaving in the streets hundreds of their dead or wounded comrades.

Many of the brave knights and soldiers of King Otto had been slain by the enemy's arrows and spears, but among the spared were Gozbert and Hildeward.

"What has happened to-day in the city of Augsburg," said the bishop to his soldiers, "is only a beginning; far fiercer and bloodier battles are yet to be fought; for the Huns will come with their whole horde, knowing how important to them is the possession of our city, where there is so much to tempt their greed; and they will also take revenge for their fallen leaders. But we have certain knowledge that King Otto is coming at quick march with a great army. May God grant us the victory!"

There was much activity in the city of Augsburg. Innumerable hands were busy repairing the walls where they were weak, or where a breach had been effected by the Huns. Great quantities of stone were broken to be thrown by hand or in slings, and great quantities of chalk were pulverized, to be thrown into the eyes of the enemy and thus to prevent them from taking aim.

The whole night they were preparing weapons and repairing those that were damaged, the bishop and his assistants helping where needed. Nuns went through the streets, singing pleading hymns, and repeating prayers to heaven for Augsburg in this dark hour. Thus the night passed.

At the first dawn of day the bishop held a service that strengthened the sad hearts with the words of the Psalmist: *Though I walk through the valley of the shadow of death, I will fear no evil; for Thou art with me, Thy rod and Thy staff, they comfort me.*

Scarcely was the service finished when the Hungarians came like a great overspreading cloud, filling the air with their wild cries and shouts as they rushed against the walls of the city with picks, crowbars, and other heavy iron tools.

But upon the walls were the men of Augsburg, and the Huns saw with alarm that they were as ready to fight as they were the previous day, and when they were struck down by arrows and stones, some of them fled, and refused to return even under the lash.

The people rejoiced with the bishop when the army led by King Otto came in sight, for they saw that the deliverance of Augsburg was assured, which had appeared hopeless to them but a moment before.

King Otto had not a large army when he set out for Augsburg, but it was greatly increased by the Bavarians. Their former leader, however, Duke Henry, was not with them, being ill at his castle at Regensburg, where he died a few weeks later.

The Franconians, under the leadership of Duke Conrad, hurried to the help of King Otto, also the Swabians and Bohemians, and when he looked upon the great number of Hungarians, he said, "Were not God on our side, we could not win this battle."

He and his army encamped on the left side of the river Lech, near Augsburg, and awaited an attack.

There Gozbert and Ruppert, twin brothers, met for the first time in many years, and it was a joyful, but serene surprise to the two gray-haired men. They clasped hands, and looked into each other's faces with the renewed affection of boyhood, after having been separated not only by time and distance, but because of their allegiance to different masters who were enemies. King Otto and Duke Henry of Bavaria. Now they were reunited in genuine brotherly love and friendship.

The four cousins also clasped hands in a common cause, Hengist and Keringer, Hildeward and Wido, all there to fight against the Huns and to protect Augsburg; and King Otto thanked God for these faithful friends.

Duke Conrad of Lorraine with his stately company of trained soldiers from beyond the Rhine hoped in this battle to atone to his father-in-law for the false step he had taken against him, and to prove that he was willing to shed his blood, if need be, in his cause.

King Otto had intended to wait for an attack from the enemy, but after the arrival of Duke Conrad and his troops it was decided to attack them the next day, August 10, 955. On the Ninth he and his whole army consecrated themselves for battle by partaking of Holy Communion and praying to God for victory over the invaders of the fatherland, calling to memory the divine promise: *Call upon Me in the day of trouble. I will deliver thee, and thou shalt glorify Me.*

On the Tenth the whole army of the Germans were on their feet, and again there was prayer to God for help, and upon his knees, with tears in his eyes, King Otto vowed that, if God gave him victory, he would found an episcopal see at Merseburg, a vow that was faithfully kept.

Deep enthusiasm prevailed among the soldiers. The orders of the leaders were obeyed most punctiliously and faithfully. They were thrilled with the one desire to win the battle and drive the barbarians for all time from German soil.

Special care was exercised in the inspection of weapons and shields, saddles and bridles, and the hoofs of the horses, that there might be no cause of failure in anyone point.

Early on the morning of the Tenth drums and trumpets sounded, and King Otto's troops marched from the camp, the flags waving in the breeze, and the rich trappings on his horse and those of knights and other noblemen gleaming in the beams of the sun.

Between the river Lech and the city of Augsburg, far up the shore, was a level plain for at least five miles, unfruitful, save for grass and weeds, a stony soil. This plain was called Lechfield. The king portioned off his army in eight parts. The first three parts were Bavarians; the fourth part was a company of Franks, led by Duke Conrad of Lorraine (or Lothringia); the fifth was led by King Otto, these being select young men, the flower of the army, who bore the banner of St. Michael; among them were Hildeward, Hengist, Keringer, and Wido. The king granted the request to allow Ruppert and Gozbert to be with them, their giant forms a head taller than the tallest, and of such weight that the largest and strongest horses were selected for them. The sixth and seventh lines were Swabians, and the eighth, the rear guard, were Bohemians.

The battle that day was beyond comparison. Some of the enemy were put to flight, but the decisive battle with the main army of the Hungarians was yet to be fought; if the Germans did not win it, all was lost. King Otto, therefore, called a halt and spoke to his men.

"You see," he said, "that we now must use our utmost strength to conquer. Not far from us, indeed, before our very eyes, stands the main strength of the enemy. But I do not fear them; should we in our own land turn our backs to the enemy? I know that they outnumber us by far, but they do not excel us in bravery and weapons; many of them do not how how to use their weapons, and many are without weapons of any kind. More than all, we have God on our side; He is our Shield and Weapon. The enemy use their weapons in wild fury, which brings no result; our weapons are used in calm faith and trust in the power and help of God.

"Truly, we should hide our heads in shame to allow Europe to see the people who conquered us and took our kingdom out of our hands. It would be far better for us to die an honorable death upon this battle-field than to be slaves under the yoke of these wild barbarians."

As the king finished his address in his calm, clear voice,

he again took up his lance and assumed his position as leader; and his soldiers proved by the fierceness of their fighting that his words had not been in vain. The Hungarians were also alert, for his words to his soldiers had another result. They recognized him as the king, and with wild cries pressed in his direction from all sides, and Bulzu, their "Prince of Princes," offered a large reward to any soldier who would put into his hands, dead or alive, the German king.

The care of the four cousins as well as that of Gozbert and Ruppert was redoubled over him, for he was in the greatest danger. Bright swords and lances flashed in the sunlight as they made their horses rear and prance about him. From all sides the Hungarians aimed for him; like hailstones came their arrows against his helmet and his coat of mail. But the king was spared, while the Huns who attacked him were reaped down like blades of grass before the scythe.

The danger to King Otto arose to the highest point when Bulzu, with high-swung curved saber, made an effort to reach him. But Gozbert and Ruppert with their clubs knocked the crowd to the ground from whence they never arose, and Ruppert dragged Bulzu from the saddle and made him his prisoner, and kept him in his iron grasp, while Gozbert used his club with deadly effect upon those coming to the assistance of their leader. Ruppert turned a moment from his prisoner, and in a flash Bulzu thrust a dagger through a fissure in his chain-coat, and Ruppert fell, mortally wounded, while Bulzu sprang upon his horse. But Gozbert was too quick for him; he dragged him from his horse, and he was again a prisoner. All this happened in a few moments of time.

Gozbert and Wido knelt beside the dying Ruppert.

"Protect the king," Ruppert said feebly. "Help him to win the battle; and Wido, I have something to tell you and to you alone. Go, Gozbert, and help protect the king!"

A battle such as was fought that day had never before been seen on German soil. The ground was covered with the dead of the Hungarians, and the waters of the Lech were red with their blood.

No quarter was given the enemy, and they must lay

down their swords, lances, battle-axes, bows, arrows, and knives. Thousands of Hungarians plunged into the river, thinking they could swim to the other side and escape; but the bank was so steep that they could not climb it in their exhausted condition, and they fell back into the river and rose no more.

The camp of the Hungarians fell into the hands of the Germans, and the prisoners were set free.

In the evening the victors met in Augsburg to estimate the heavy loss of life the German army had sustained. Many noblemen were among the brave men who had fallen, among them Diethold, brother of Bishop Adalrich, and Duke Conrad of Lorraine; and many faithful personal friends in humbler positions, among them Steward Ruppert, who had saved the king's life from the curved saber of the prince of the Huns.

Duke Conrad had lost his life on the field. While raising his helmet, an arrow from the enemy pierced his throat, and he fell from his horse, mortally wounded. His great longing had been to atone for his rebellion against the king, and his wish was fulfilled, for it was through him that the great victory had been obtained.

It was a great victory, but the king's heart was heavy. "He gave me much sorrow," he said mournfully, speaking of Duke Conrad, "but he has done all in his power to atone for it. A man of nobler character never lived, and his loss will be a sad remembrance all my days."

In all the churches of the kingdom services were held in which the Lord was praised for having given the fatherland this victory.

17

❧ After Many Days ❧

WHILE THE HUNGARIANS were in wild flight and the Germans rejoiced over the great victory, Wido was kneeling beside Ruppert, whose life was ebbing away; and tears of sorrow for the one who so loved him, and whom he so loved, could not be stayed; for he saw that the wounded man, though regaining consciousness, could not live.

"Tell me of the battle, Wido," Ruppert said feebly. "Did the king win?"

"Yes, father; it is a glorious victory. All the Hungarians have fled except the wounded and the dead, and they are many."

"Thank the Almighty for this! Now listen, Wido, to something I will tell you, for I have but little time to live. For many years we lived in Hungary, and my dear wife and I and our little boy of two years lived happily in our cabin. Then, as now, there were attacks made upon German lands, and we returned with much booty. Just before we set out upon one of these invasions, a terrible trouble came to us. Our little Wido died after a short illness, and my wife was almost beside herself with grief."

"Had I a brother of the same name as myself?" asked Wido in astonishment.

"Do not interrupt me," pleaded Ruppert. "I have but little time to live, and have much to say that lies heavy upon my heart.

"I was compelled to leave my wife in the loneliness of

our cabin and grieving for our boy. On our return to Hungary I shortened my walk to the cabin by a cross-way leading through the forest, and while passing along, my mind filled with the thought of the loneliness in our home without our boy, I heard the cry of a child. I hurried to the thicket from where the sound came, and found a little boy of about the age of our Wido, and clad in the dress worn by German children. I tried to comfort him, but he could only say, "Father, mother, poor Arnulf!"

"Arnulf!" exclaimed Wido, "that was the name of the little brother of Hengist and Keringer who was stolen by the Hungarians when the robbers burned the castle of Gerhard von Stein."

"Yes, but do not interrupt me; my time is short. The wounded soldier beside him had only strength to tell me that I could do nothing for him, but begged me to take the child to his wife, who loved children and was childless, and he had taken it as a prisoner from a castle named Eberstein, which they had robbed and burned. His home was three miles out of the way, but I made the promise and kept it, and when he had ceased to breathe, I covered him with dry twigs and leaves, and kept on my way to his cabin.

"His wife was deeply distressed to hear of her husband's death, but refused to take the child, as she was not able to support it now that she was alone in the world, and so I took little Arnulf to my home, and the love we had for our Wido we now showed him, and also gave him our own boy's name."

"Has it come to your mind that Gerhard von Stein is my father and Hengist and Keringer my brothers?" asked Wido in a trembling voice.

"Yes, and there is not the least doubt about it."

"How wonderful, how wonderful!" ejaculated the young man in a tone of awe.

"Yes, it is one of the things in which we see that God has been our guide that I, as steward of Beleke Castle, lay wounded and near death by the brook, and that Hengist and Keringer took me up, placed me upon a horse, and took me to Hartrun Castle. There I lay for weeks, out of my mind from fever, and there Gerhard von Stein and his sons waited upon me as if I were the most faithful of friends instead of a known enemy.

"It was because of my love for you, and for no other reason, that I kept the knowledge to myself that you are a son of Gerhard von Stein. Once at Hartrun, when recovering from my sickness, I was on the point of telling him the secret; but the thought came to me that I could not endure living without you; that I must live alone, while Gerhard von Stein would be blessed with three noble sons to cheer his old age. But to a monk in whom I have every confidence I have given a parchment upon which is the whole story, and which will be given you after my death. If you and your father think I have done wrong by keeping it a secret, remember that it was my love for you that prompted it."

"Dear father," said Wido, "there is no one upon earth to whom I owe more than to you; next to God you have been my benefactor, and it is to you and to my dear foster-mother that I owe my life. I would have died in the forest, had you not found me, and cared for me as your own son ever since."

"Your words cheer my heart," said Ruppert feebly; "they relieve it of a burden which has oppressed it; and I hope your father and brothers will forgive me for keeping you from them so long."

Their conversation was interrupted by the sound of hoofs, and to Wido's joy they were his foster-uncle Gozbert, Hildeward, Hengist, and Keringer. His heart thrilled at the surprise it would be to them to know that he was a brother to two of them instead of a cousin.

Ruppert revived sufficiently to tell them the story. They had never suspected it, but heard it with delight that one so loved was their own dear elder brother.

"Bless you, bless you all!" whispered Ruppert feebly. "Oh, Gozbert, the same loving Father has given our king and fatherland victory over their enemies; praise be to His holy name!"

Silently and with tear-dimmed eyes the little company gathered about the dying soldier. His life soon ebbed away; that evening the body of the faithful servant of his God, his king, and his fatherland was laid to rest in the fragrant forest.

This duty done, they kept on their way to Regensburg to tell the king all that had transpired since he left the battle-field for Duke Henry's castle.

Regensburg was celebrating the glorious victory over the Huns, and King Otto rejoiced with them; yet his heart was heavy because of the dangerous illness of his brother, Duke Henry.

He was grieved to hear of the death of Ruppert, though knowing before leaving the battle-field that he could not live. He was surprised and pleased to hear that Wido was now Arnulf, the lost son of Gerhard von Stein.

On November 1, but a few weeks after the battle of Augsburg, Duke Henry of Bavaria was called from earth and was buried from the Church of Our Lady in Regensburg.

He had always been the favorite son of his mother, Queen Matilda, and from the depths of her stricken heart she uttered the prayer: *O God, have mercy upon the soul of Thy servant who has been called by Thee from this life. Consider the few pleasures he has had upon earth, and how many of his days have been filled with trouble and grief.*

The time had now come for the young men to return to Hartrun, and King Otto gave them a word of advice at parting.

"It is well for you," he said, "to return to your father. He is growing old, and will rejoice to receive the son whom he had given up for lost. You are all worthy sons of a worthy father. Return to Hartrun, and cultivate the land diligently as an example to the young men of Saxony. I will add more land to that estate, which is already of many acres, and there will be plenty of employment for you three brothers.

"No; you do not owe me any thanks," he said, as they tried to give voice to their gratitude; "for it is impossible for me to repay you for what you have done for me and mine."

"Before we go, I will ask your Majesty about Prince Ludolph," said Hildeward. "My heart is warm toward the one who was my beloved superior, and for whom I have the love of a humble friend."

"Ludolph did not battle with us against the Hungarians, for he has gone to battle against the Wends, and I wish one of you faithful and companionable von Steins were with him. Hildeward, perhaps you will be willing to go?"

"I shall be glad, indeed, to go," exclaimed Hildeward in delight, "and I am sure that Uncle Gozbert will go with us beyond the Elbe to fight the Wends. On our way we can stop for a short visit at the monastery to see Abbot Martin."

"I heartily agree to this," said the king. "Abbot Martin did me and mine a great service, which I can never repay."

With the kind farewell of the king they left Regensburg to go their separate ways, hoping to meet again.

It was impossible to describe the surprise and delight with which Gerhard von Stein welcomed his eldest son, his Arnulf, and he gave thanks to God, who had so blessed him.

In the meantime Gozbert and Hildeward had reached the monastery, and there was much of interest to be spoken of since they had parted, and there was great rejoicing over the victory.

Leaving the monastery, they kept on their way to aid Prince Ludolph, who was doing his best to conquer the Wends, and thus atone for his rebellion against his father.

In the meantime King Otto had in his mind a commission for his son, which, he was sure, would be gladly accepted, and in June, 956, when Ludolph returned, having completely conquered the Wends, he told him of it.

"You remember, Ludolph," he said, "that at the meeting of our parliament in August, 951, at Augsburg, Berengarius and his son Adelbert promised to give the vassal oath of allegiance to me. This promise he has never fulfilled; for as soon as he returned to Italy, he hurried to call together the bishops, princes, counts, and other members of the nobility among the Italians, and censured them for their lapse of fealty to them.

"He would not have dared to do this, had I not been too much engaged here in those wars for the protection of our kingdom to demand by force of arms the keeping of his promise.

"But since then times have changed. Thank God, I am now in a position to show to Berengarius and his son that the sovereignty of Italy is not in their hands, but in mine. I have decided to send a strong army to bring the disobedient, covenant-breaking people to account; and I will place you at the head of the army as commander-in-chief."

"Oh, my good, kind father!" cried Ludolph in delighted surprise. "How noble it is in you to entrust me with such a commission; I feel now that I have atoned for my shameful rebellion against you."

"It is truly no binding agreement, my son, but I will so consider it, and if you bring this commission to a perfect ending, I will make you king of Italy as a recompense for the loss of the Duchy of Swabia. I am sure," he added, with a smile, "that King of Italy sounds better than Duke of Swabia."

"Dear father, how can I ever be grateful enough to you! I shall again have place among my friends; for all who were loyal to you have deserted me, which is just what I deserve. But this will prove that you trust me, and I can again hold up my head among them; for the one whom the king honors will be honored among men."

These were the happy words that passed his lips, and his father was glad to see the change in his son's sad face and manner. He also knew that the change from his aimless existence to one of interested activity was a necessity to one of his temperament.

"Now," he said, "lose no time in calling your troops together. You must cross the Alps while it is summer. May the Almighty guide you and be your shelter and protection."

New life was now pulsating in Ludolph's sad heart. His friends flocked to his standard, loyal to him now that he was at peace with the king. In the early part of July he and his troops had crossed the Alps and went to Verona, and from there to Pavia.

Hildeward was his chosen companion, and rode by his side throughout the long journey, and they never wearied of each other's company.

Berengarius was not ignorant of this new danger to his

position as king. In great haste he and Adelbert collected an army and led it against Ludolph, who, upon reaching Italian soil, was joined by a good number of the enemies of Berengarius, so that his army was greatly increased.

The battle was on. Ludolph was victorious, and Pavia was in his hands. But this did not discourage Adelbert and his father. In the second battle Adelbert led his troops, but again Ludolph was successful, and Berengarius and his son were compelled to flee to a place of safety. The whole kingdom of Italy rejoiced at this turn of events.

Master of the situation, Ludolph acted with mildness and discretion and with friendliness toward all. Even his enemies admired him, while he was loved by his own soldiers.

Ludolph would have been happy, could he have reached the aim his father had planned for him; but it was not the will of the Almighty that he should be king of Italy. On the third of September, 957, he went with his dear friend Hildeward to Pombia, a place in the province of Novara near Lake Maggiore. He contracted a fever, and often he lay unconscious for hours.

Hildeward was his constant attendant, being with him night and day. He greatly feared that he whom he loved so dearly would never again see his dear father and his home. Ludolph blamed himself for having given his father trouble, and Hildeward did all he could to comfort him, assuring him that he had been fully forgiven.

"My dear father forgave me when I transgressed so terribly against him," said the young prince feebly, "and I believe that my heavenly Father will forgive me — and I shall see — my — Savior." Lisping feebly a few more words of reliance upon his Lord, he passed away, a smile of content resting upon his pale lips.

Prince Ludolph had won the love of the people, and there was great lamentation throughout the country when it became known that he would never be their king.

His German soldiers, knowing of his love for the fatherland, resolved that he should rest there instead of in foreign soil; and a detachment of strong men, for love of him, united to carry him across the Alps to his home in Saxony.

They chose the shortest route, but it was also the steepest; it was a long and difficult journey. No one, however, considered it to be anything but a sad and loving duty which they felt honored to perform for one they had loved so much. They took turns in resting on the way, Hildeward doing his share in helping. At length they reached Germany, and passed on to Mayence, where the burial was to take place. Never was a prince more sincerely mourned.

Through Hildeward the king heard of his son's last days in Italy and of his peaceful passing away, which was of unspeakable comfort to the mourning father.

"I can never repay you," he said one day after he had recovered his composure in some measure, "but I will do what I think will be of the most lasting benefit and happiness to you, and to your uncle Gozbert, who has been so faithful to me and my cause.

"I know that in your veins is the blood of the forester and the hunter, and the gift of land in field and forest is what would suit you best.

"Not far from Polde, at the foot of the Harz Mountains, is a tract of land of five hundred acres; I wish to give this to you. It is now unfruitful, because uncultivated, but your diligent and intelligent care of it will make it a garden-spot. A large forest belongs to it, in which is an abundance of nuts and wild fruits, and plenty of game. Between the fields and forest there is a hunting-lodge, roomy, and furnished with all things needed for use and comfort, as well as for hunting; and the lodge and all it contains goes to you with the land and the forest. This property is for you and your heirs for all time. I have but one condition to make, and that is, that your uncle Gozbert share your home for life; together you will have the comforts of a happy home."

"It is too much, too much for what I have done," said Hildeward with tears of gratitude.

"No, I feel I can never repay you for what you have done for me and mine. My beloved Ludolph, now safely at home in his Father's house, you once delivered from certain death in the forest, and the service you rendered Queen Adelheid in helping her escape from prison and danger can never be fully estimated. May God reward you, for I never can.

"To your uncle Gozbert I owe much for his faithful service. He well deserves a home in his old age as a gift; and with no one would he be as happy as with you."

Hildeward's sincere gratitude was freely expressed as King Otto put the parchment into his hand which secured the new home to him.

Gozbert's heart was filled with sweet content on hearing that he was to share the home with his beloved Hildeward, a home such as he had never dreamed of getting.

Before they took possession, Hildeward went to visit his sister Hedwig, who, with Queen Adelheid, was at the castle at Quedlinburg. It was a happy meeting.

In the autumn of 961, King Otto, accompanied by Queen Adelheid and a number of the members of the German nobility, journeyed to Rome, called there by Pope John XII, to protect him against Berengarius.

Otto rescued the pope from his danger, and was rewarded by the pope with the long-wished-for honor — the imperial crown of the Caesars. While in Rome, he was crowned.

The coronation was a splendid festival.

The king left his castle on Mont Mario on a spirited white horse, and surrounded by bishops, cardinals, and members of the German and Italian nobility, all in splendid array, and their horses richly caparisoned, made a beautiful sight as they passed through the streets of Rome to St. Peter's Church.

The pope awaited them there, and with much ceremony King Otto and Queen Adelheid were crowned February 2, 962.

Four years later he again visited Rome, taking with him the queen and their young son Otto, six years of age, who was anointed and crowned by the pope, receiving the title of Otto II. This was done that the claim of the royal House of Saxony to the throne might have the sanction of the Church.

The last Imperial Diet of King Otto was held in Quedlinburg, Saxony, in June, 973, and was a brilliant gathering.

In the same year he visited Merseburg and Memleben, where his father Henry had passed away, and there King Otto's brilliant and eventful life was ended. He was buried at Merseburg.

He had reached the age of sixty-one. Thirty-seven years he had been ruler of Germany, and twelve years of the thirty-seven he had also been ruler of the Holy Roman Empire.

His reign was considered the golden age of Germany, his title being Otto the Great.

His beloved and pious queen Adelheid departed this life in 999, in a cloister which she had founded in Alsace, and there she rests in a tomb.

Hedwig von Stein, her beloved lady-in-waiting, was with her to the last. After her death she went to Polde, at the foot of the Harz Mountains, where she shared her brother's home. After many years and many experiences this brother and sister were again under one roof as in their childhood, in their cottage on the river in Burgundy.

With Hildeward and his wife and children she was contented and happy, as they were to have her with them.

Uncle Gozbert had passed away years before, and was laid to rest in the beautiful forest he loved in life.

The quelling of the Hungarians by King Otto the Great was not only a blessing to the Germans, but was a turning-point in the history of the Hungarians.

They gradually gave up their wild, fierce, warlike, and wandering life, and having the peaceful, industrious, and home-loving Germans as an example, they settled in fixed homes, and became amenable to the laws and rules of Christian living.

Made in United States
Orlando, FL
11 September 2024

51385055R10085